Copyright © 2024 Holly Green

All rights reserved

The characters and events portrayed in this book fictitious. Any similarity to real persons, living or dead, is coincidental and not intended by the author.

No part of this book may be reproduced, or stored in a retrieval system, or transmitted in any form or by any means, electronic, mechanical, photocopying, recording, or otherwise, without express written permission of the publisher.

ISBN: 9798868021657

Printed in the United Kingdom

For Emma, the strongest woman I know.
Here's to another 20 years of friendship.

Chapter One

Mia carefully placed the last frosted cherry on one of the three cakes in front of her and stepped back to critique her handiwork.

Every time she said yes to a cake commission she couldn't wait to see how it would turn out. However at the same time as saying yes, she'd immediately begin to fret about the very same project. For weeks she'd plan and draw. Scrapping ideas, trawling the internet for inspiration and reaching a fevered point where she'd believe there would be no way she could convert the design in her head into a real life version.

Then, after a few days of baking, creating and icing she'd somehow manage to produce something she'd be incredibly proud of, even going so far as to post a few photos on her Instagram page, which in turn would lead to more enquiries and a waiting list. And, eventually, the cycle of worry and excitement would begin again. Mia couldn't help but smile at the process, which would send her slightly mad each time but that she wouldn't give up for anything. It brought her immense joy to see her customer's reactions and to be a part of their celebrations. Weddings, birthday, anniversaries; even on one occasion a four tier spectacle to celebrate a very loved dog's eighth birthday. Mia accepted all commissions, and worried about all of them equally.

Today, the early January sunshine eased gently through the bakery's windows onto the space she was working and highlighted the crisply white iced cake. Delicate frosted cherries glistening with sugar cascaded down each of the three tiers, the light causing them to sparkle. An intricate Japanese cherry blossom design Mia had hand painted in edible inks wound its way across the rest of the crisp icing canvas. It was a design to reflect that the soon-to-be married couple had met in Japan.

Ellie, Mia's best friend and joint owner of their café and bakery *Tiers of Joy*, came in from the kitchen holding a tray of their bestselling cinnamon rolls and began to arrange them on decorative wooden boards near to the till. Not that they'd stay for long, they sold more cinnamon rolls than anything else.

'That's your best yet,' she said, looking over at the cakes Mia had just finished.

'You say that every time.' Mia said smiling. Very carefully she began to place each of the three cakes into individual boxes. When she reached the wedding venue she'd dowel them so they'd stand as one three-tier cake. Just as she closed the final box, taking care not to smudge the delicate design, there was a shout of irritation from Ellie causing Mia to look over as sheaves of baby pink paper fluttered from the till drawer to the blue slate floor. Mia knelt down to scoop up the many little notelets, catching sight of handwriting which caused her throat to constrict as she fought off tears.

Ellie knelt down beside her and put an arm around her shoulder. 'Why are you hanging on to these?'

Mia shrugged, staring blankly at her hands full of notes. 'I guess I didn't have the heart to throw them away,' she said.

'Much like you didn't have the heart to ask him to pay,' Ellie chided affectionately. The two women stood up and paused for a moment as they looked at the multiple notes Mia was holding, each signed *Albert* with a flourish. After a moment's pause Ellie gently squeezed Mia's hand. 'Keep them if they make you happy, just maybe not in the till drawer.'

Mia nodded and thrust them into her apron pockets, blinking a couple of times to clear her tears. They didn't come so readily now, but they still appeared when she least expected them.

'Are you delivering the cake, or is someone coming? It'll be the morning rush soon.' Ellie broke into her thoughts, looking meaningfully at the clock on the wall opposite, whilst she flicked the coffee machine on and began to empty a bag of coffee beans into it, sending a waft of nutty, caramelised scent into the air.

'I need to deliver it, but I'll be back soon; it's only up the road. I wouldn't leave you to the rush on your own now would I?' Mia said, grinning at her friend. Before Ellie could reply, Mia began to lift the boxes of cake into a larger plastic box, something which would make it easier for her to take to her car. 'Sam should be here soon, she'll be able to help.'

Both the women shook their heads, trying not to laugh. Sam was their 60-year-old assistant who did more talking than working, but who had been with them since they'd opened their business 18 months ago and had a heart of gold. She was popular with the regulars, even though she liked to talk non-stop which caused a queue to go towards the door most mornings.

Mia lifted the large plastic box up and made her way to the door, struggling a little with the weight but knowing one false move would mean the cakes would be ruined. Ellie opened the door for Mia, letting Liam from the grocers in as she did so. The two disappeared within the shop and Mia shivered at the chill of the outside compared to the warmth of her cosy café. She looked back through the window and smiled at the sight. It never got old seeing her own café, the lights giving a welcoming orange glow in contrast to the grey outside, and plenty of snuggly sofas to sink into once hot drinks and cake orders had been decided upon. Turning back to the chilly morning she carefully took the box to her car, a bright red Mini Cooper parked opposite the café, nicknamed Rose.

She was 20 year's old and held together with little more than super glue and hope but Mia could never be persuaded to sell, or worse, scrap the car. The old girl and her had been together for over 15 years, and she wasn't going to break up with her longest relationship. Rose had been far more reliable than any man she'd dated.

Until recently.

Recently the car had been showing signs of age and Mia regularly sent up a small prayer of thanks when it started first time. Forcing the passenger door open as the cold late January temperatures had caused it to seize, she secured the cake box in the passenger seat and quickly got into the driver's side. Debating whether she should have the radio or the heating on; the two didn't work at the same time anymore, Mia settled on music as she didn't want the cake to overheat. She negotiated her way out of the tight parking space, driving carefully over the cobbled streets which paved Mistlebrook, the picturesque English market town she'd lived in since she was 10, whilst holding her breath at the particularly bumpy bits that asked a lot of Rose's suspension.

Other than the perilous cobbles and one cyclist who thought he could race her car off the traffic lights, Mia made it to Shawford Manor, a large house of faded grandeur on the outskirts of the town, without injury to her or the cakes.

It was a shame, Mia pondered, but lately there'd been fewer and fewer weddings at the house. Swallowing down the nerves that always came with entering the manor, there was something so imposing about it, Mia tried to pick up the large plastic box that contained the cakes from the passenger seat to carry indoors.

The box only just fitted the space in the car and had become wedged between the seat and the gearstick. The door didn't want to stay open so Mia awkwardly attempted to use her thigh to keep the car door from closing whilst pulling the box free. Instead, the door closed shut, managing to catch her bright red coat in just as she lifted the box out, trapping her.

'Allow me.' A voice from behind startled her, causing Mia to jump but she held onto the box. A tall, dark haired man, dressed for the outdoors in a knee length green overcoat and wellies, accompanied by a black Labrador, appeared at her side. He quickly reopened the door, allowing Mia to stand aside, then took the box easily from her, shutting the door, calling the dog to heel and rescuing Mia in one fluid movement.

'Are we going to the house?' he called over his shoulder as he made his way in that direction.

Mia recovered herself and walked quickly across the gravel driveway to catch up, matching the man's strides as the two climbed the Georgian cream stone steps of the grand house. She went slightly ahead of him to open the heavy oak door and stood aside so he could make his way through.

'Thank you, that's really helpful. I'd got myself in a bit of a pickle. I really should work out a better way of transporting cakes, I probably need a new car to be honest,' Mia laughed a little too loudly and told herself to quieten down. She could tell she was babbling but it was something she always did when there were uncomfortable silences. Keeping her mouth shut, she walked ahead of him down the highly decorated hallway which was hung with oil paintings of previous owners and showed him to the large reception room where she was setting up. He placed the box on a white cloth covered table whilst Mia hovered nearby, fizzing with worry that he may have somehow caused some damage to the contents inside. As soon as he moved away from the box Mia opened it to check the cakes had survived and breathed with relief when she saw all three were fine. She looked back smiling to thank the man for his help. But he had, it seemed, vanished without a trace.

'Bye then,' she muttered under her breath, focusing her attention on the cakes. They still needed to be stacked, ribbons attached and the accessories added to the top. Casting off her coat and throwing it to the side so she could focus on finishing up the cake and getting back to the café, Mia realised in her haste to get the box out of the car she'd left her bag with all the extra bits, such as ribbons and dowels, in it. She blew out a breath of frustration but knew she'd need to pop out to get them. Quickly Mia made her way to the Mini, collected her bag and returned to the room.

As soon as she got to the table Mia realised something was different and her heart leapt a little. There, trapped by one of the boxes, as though thrown from a distance, a small pink slip of paper lay on the table. Her heart quickening, Mia moved slowly afraid of what it would say. This was impossible, surely?

She picked up the paper in the shape of a heart and couldn't help it. She smiled at what it said.

Chapter Two

'How about one of our choccy fudge doo-dahs?' Sam suggested to Tony, the owner of the butchers, who, as far as Mia and Ellie were concerned, only ever came to their café as he had an enormous crush on their assistant.

'Hmm, that's tempting, would you have one with me? I'm buying,' Tony said, wafting his card at the till and smiling with a lopsided grin. Ellie nudged Mia, who was icing some cinnamon rolls and nodded in the older couple's direction.

Sam shook her head ruefully. 'Oh no, I don't have any of them now, terrible for my waistline working here.' She leant against the wooden counter, plating up Tony's brownie. 'In fact, shall I let you in on a secret?'

The man moved as close as he could with a counter between them and smiled. 'I'm ready for your secrets Sam.'

'I've been for hypnosis over at Mystic Ruth's,' she nodded in the direction of the shop which sold incense sticks and fossils, alongside runes and tarot cards. 'She hypnotised me to never eat sugar and it worked. I haven't wanted anything sweet since she did it last week.' She paused, looking away slightly with a far off gaze. 'But I eat my weight in cheese now.'

Mia heard Ellie snort back a laugh, then quickly cover it up as she turned to serve Tony his coffee.

'Your soya latte, extra foam,' she said, breaking the spell which Sam had cast on Tony, causing him to jump a little and in the process spilling some of the hot drink on the counter. 'Don't worry, I'll sort it, and we'll pop a treat on your table as a way of apologising,' she grinned, wiping the side down.

Tony smiled dreamily. 'No need to apologise. I'm happy to sit at this table with the best view in Mistlebrook.' Sam rolled her eyes and turned her attention to the next customer in line.

'What can I get you, love?'

'Actually, I was hoping to talk to,' the voice broke off and Mia looked up, wondering who was talking. As she did so, her heart caught in her mouth, it was the man from the house. The one who'd helped her a few days ago when she was in need, then disappeared before she could thank him. Wiping her hands on a cloth and turning to place the freshly iced cinnamon rolls behind the glass fronted display area, Mia smiled up at him. Today, gone were the waterproofs and wet weather gear, in their place was a chunky grey jumper, with a beaten up leather jacket slung over the top. His hair was lightly ruffled from the early January breeze outside. He coughed, bringing her back to her senses.

'I just...ah...' he ran his hands through his dark hair and grinned as though caught out. 'I came to say sorry for disappearing on you like that and to introduce myself properly.' As he stuck his hand out to Mia the sleeve of his leather jacket caught one of the sticky iced rolls and it was knocked onto the floor. His face was a picture of horror and his leather jacket had icing up the sleeve. 'Oh, damn and blast,' he began wiping at the icing with a small serviette Mia had handed him, causing her to giggle a little.

'Damn and blast?' she repeated, raising her eyebrow.

He shook his head. 'I've spent too long with my mother, her sayings must have rubbed off on me. Before anything else happens, hi, I'm Will.'

'Mia.'

'I know. I've done my research on you,' he grinned, then shook his head as though catching himself. 'That is, I've done my research on you two and your business, and I've got a proposition for you. Can we talk?' he stuttered a little, which endeared him more to Mia and she felt her stomach flip. Will nodded to the back of the café, where squashy sofas and reading lamps had been positioned so their customers felt at home. There was even a community library, somewhere for the locals to drop off books they'd enjoyed and swap them for someone else's.

Mia looked behind her to see if Ellie had heard the conversation, she hadn't mentioned bumping into Will to her friend. Partly because the meeting was so swift it barely merited a mention, and also because she'd sworn off men after...well...after *that*...and Ellie would make sure she stuck to it. Not least because she'd joined Mia in the 'no man' pact for a year. So not even a country gent could change her mind. Not even a country gent who looked oh so good in a pair of faded Levis and had the deepest blue eyes she'd ever seen.

Ellie was busy serving Liam, the grocer's son. In the 18 months they'd been running the café Mia wasn't certain she'd heard more than five words from him. He preferred to be served by Sam or Ellie than her and though she'd been put-out when they'd first opened that he'd taken a disliking to her, he was a regular so she did her best to be pleasant. Catching his eye, she smiled. 'Morning Liam, you're later than usual.' He made some sort of grunt which she translated to being a response and she turned to Ellie. 'I'm just going to take my break and, erm, talk to a customer. But let me know if you need anything.'

Ellie looked in the direction where Will had sat down and raised her eyebrows at Mia, but didn't say anything, just smiled and nodded her head then continued making Liam's coffee.

Rolling her eyes, Mia ignored her friend. They'd known each other for so long she knew what Ellie's meaningful glance meant and in a bid to help the blush which was creeping its' way over her face subside she busied herself in pulling together some drinks and cakes to bring over to Will. Once she was sure she wasn't quite so red, Mia brought the tray over.

'I didn't know what you'd like, but went for a straightforward Americano and I thought you'd enjoy one of these which hasn't attached itself to your jacket,' Mia explained as she brought a tray over to the low coffee table next to the sofa he'd chosen, placing a plate of cinnamon rolls down.

'I'm more of a tea guy to be honest. Sorry, silly joke. This looks great,' Will grinned and patted the seat next to him. Mia hesitated. 'Come on, I won't bite.' He lightly pulled her arm and flashed a grin. Unless I want him to, Mia thought, a little hungrily. As though to demonstrate a point he bit into the cinnamon roll. Mia pushed all thoughts of biting out of her mind and sat down on the sofa but as close to the arm of the chair as possible.

Mia took a sip of her own coffee and waited for Will's proposition. The silence between them was broken with the sounds of the coffee machine grinding up beans, and occasional bouts of steam shushing from the counter.

'So?' She prompted. She didn't want to leave Ellie and Sam for too long especially as the Red Hat Society ladies had arrived. A group of women aged 50+ who weren't quite WI material and who could often be found on jaunts to London, or wine tasting in the local restaurants. They stood out with their red hats in varying designs, including berets, felt hats and woolly ones, all of which contrasted heavily with their purple coats, scarves and dresses. The women were a lot of fun, but could also be guaranteed to take over the majority of the café; and needed plenty of tea and cakes.

'Sorry, I'm keeping you; this is a busy place, isn't it?' Will said as he watched Tony vacate his table and chivalrously offer it to one of the older members of the red hatted group.

Mia smiled. 'It is but we have a lot of competition.' She turned to look Will in the eyes, which she regretted immediately as he held her stare, causing her stomach to do all manner of gymnastic moves her body couldn't manage. She broke the moment by looking away. 'We're always having to push to make it to the end of each month. We just don't have the backing, like the chains do. We're more expensive because we're independent, but that's because we make everything on site, or buy in from super local.' She shrugged. She wasn't sure why she was admitting her business woes to this almost stranger.

'That's why you do wedding cakes then?'

Mia cocked her head to one side thoughtfully. 'Sort of. It's the thing I love the most making cakes for other people's big days. I love the creativity and yes I can make a little extra for the business but mainly it's for me. It's what I'm most passionate about.' Yet again she wondered where this openness was coming from. Usually she kept herself as a closed book, one of the many things which she was certain had caused her previous relationship to break down.

'I own Shawford Manor,' Will began, and Mia sucked in her breath.

'You do? I thought it was owned by the council?'

Will shook his head. 'It's been on loan to them, my father didn't want to manage it but I want to give it a go. I think I could make it a great business, a really successful one. I can see events there; parties, special nights. I'm looking to launch everything with a Valentine's ball; that's where you come in.' He stopped and looked deeply at Mia, his enthusiasm was making his eyes sparkle.

'Me?' She wondered if now would be the right time to explain that she'd sworn off men for a year.

'Yes, I'm looking for someone to help me organise the ball; there's a lot to do and we've only got a few weeks. I need someone who knows the area and can make sure I'm not being taken advantage of.'

'But what about the events planners?' Mia had been working with the women at Shawford Manor the past five years, bringing wedding ideas to life. She'd been making wedding cakes before Ellie came to her with the idea of *Tiers of Joy* and the two had begun their baking venture. Combining Mia with her baking background and Ellie's obsessions with good food and even better coffee.

Will shook his head and Mia watched as a trace of embarrassment seemed to etch itself across his features. 'They've gone too. You must have noticed how few weddings have been there lately? People just don't think of it as a destination anymore and as soon as I took over the manor, they were both moved by the council elsewhere. So I'm starting from scratch.'

'It's a big project. But I can imagine the manor would look wonderful dressed for a ball; I've only ever seen it for wedding receptions,' Mia said, her mind whirring with thoughts of big dresses, string quartets and people dancing like they did in the period dramas she enjoyed watching. Maybe Mr Darcy would arrive.

'What theme would you do?' Will asked, then took a deep sip of coffee.

Distracted from her Darcy based daydream Mia looked over at the red hatted women and smiled. They'd been telling her about an event they'd attended the year before that she'd wished she could have gone to. She turned back to Will, still beaming. 'I'd love a masked ball. There's something so exciting about everyone in their masks and not knowing who everyone else is. We'd have a dress code; it would be black tie and everyone would be encouraged to wear Valentines themed colours, like red and pink. Oh, and there'd be flowers everywhere,' she said, her eyes lighting up with the idea of the finished ball. Mia was getting the same sense of anticipation of organising the ball and coming up with ideas, as she did with her cake commissions.

Will smiled at her enthusiasm. 'Yes, that's perfect. It's a great way of announcing that Shawford Manor is back and ready for business.'

They stared at each other and when Will leant forward, Mia instinctively did the same. Her heart racing, watching the way his pupils dilated as they neared her, she she wondered what he was going to do. That is until she watched as he leant past her for his coffee and returned to the safety of the other side of the sofa. Her heart hammered in her chest, and she could feel her cheeks flaming. Mia swallowed her own drink quickly and hoped he hadn't noticed anything.

'So, when can I have you?'

Mia's coffee went the wrong way and she began to splutter and cough uncontrollably. Tears forced themselves from her eyes and, she realised at the same time as it happened, two snot trails slimed down onto her lips. Just as she was noting the many ways she'd embarrassed herself, Will slammed his hand hard on her back, causing her to emit the loudest burp she'd ever managed.

Mortified, her face wet with coffee and snot, and to a now very quiet café, Mia turned, as gracefully as she could to Will and accepted the paper napkin he was offering to wipe it all away. She coughed a little and the last piece of coffee dislodged itself from her lungs.

'Sorry about that episode,' she whispered, her throat sore from coughing. Self-consciously she tucked a lock of dark blonde hair back under the baseball cap she wore to keep her mass of curls out of the way whilst working and tried to regain a modicum of composure.

Will's face, which had until that point remained impassive as stone, broke out into the largest grin.

'It's not quite the reaction I want from someone who's going to work with me. That is, if you still want to? Hopefully you're still open to the possibility?' He offered her another paper napkin.

Convinced Will would withdraw his offer following the coughing debacle and embarrassingly aware she'd read the wrong thing into what he'd said, Mia breathed a deep sigh of relief. She needed the extra work. The café wasn't doing enough to sustain itself and sooner or later, she and Ellie would have to face facts that they just weren't going to see another year in business without some sort of divine intervention.

'It's a yes from me. How about I come up with a few ideas, and I visit you in two days' time? Then we can go over everything that's needed and get the promotion agreed; you've not got long until February 14th. You'll want a sell-out.'

Will drained his coffee and placed the cup into the saucer.

'It's a date,' he grinned at her, shook her hand then stood up and walked out of the café leaving Mia perplexed. He was offering her a job, a dream job she knew she'd be good at.

So why did it feel like there was a catch?

Chapter Three

'Cheers,' Ellie said they clinked glasses and saw away their third passionfruit martini. They were in their favourite booth of the cocktail and piano bar, *Florida Keys*, which had opened in the eighties and never seen fit to change its décor. The neon signs on the walls included bright green palm trees, luminescent pink flamingos and a red piano, along with a very ornate gold sign that declared *play life to your own tune* that hung behind the bar.

The one thing the owners did stay up to date with was the pianist's music. And the cocktail list.

As a piano version of Miley Cyrus' *Flowers* played out from the corner, Mia leant back into the deep burgundy velvet of the booth and downed her shot of prosecco that accompanied her sweet pink cocktail. Her head was feeling fuzzy and she knew tomorrow was going to hurt. She'd need to be baking by 5am.

If she stopped drinking now she might *just* be able to manage to get the usual loaves and rolls in before Ellie arrived at her usual time of 6am. At this point the two would work methodically together – a dance of sorts – weighing and mixing and decorating the rest of the day's bakes. Usually they'd make at least three 'hero' cakes, such as coffee and walnut, along some smaller bakes such as cupcakes, muffins and of course their cinnamon rolls.

But as Ellie indicated to the barman for two more drinks, Mia came to the conclusion that tomorrow was not going to be fun. Or easy.

Ellie snorted for the hundredth time. 'I couldn't believe it. Snot was *everywhere*. EVERYWHERE. What did he say to you? I haven't seen you make as much of a fool out of yourself in years,' she held her sides as though she couldn't prevent the amount of mirth from spilling out of her.

Shaking her head and grinning at her own misadventure, Mia stuck a tongue out at Ellie. 'Thanks. I can always count on you for support. As if I need reminding what an idiot I made out of myself. Anyway, he was offering me a job, a bit of extra work. I'm going to be organising a masked ball.' Mia sipped the last dregs of her martini and watched as a waitress brought the new ones over.

Ellie squealed a little. 'Oh I've never been to one of those. I can come, right?'

Mia laughed. 'When were you never invited to something? Of course you're coming. Though it might just be us there,' she admitted. Her fears which had been simmering below the surface since Will had left the coffee that morning were finally being allowed to run free with the encouragement of some alcohol.

'Oh tsk. You'll do an incredible job with this. He knows it, I know it. You just need to believe in yourself. Let's toast, to getting work and hanging out with hot, unattainable men,' Ellie clinked her glass against Mia's grinning. Pink liquid sloshed over the sides of the glasses coating Mia's hand in a sticky goo.

'Unattainable?' Mia asked, wiping a napkin over her hand as best she could, looking at Ellie for an explanation.

Ellie put her head to one side and smiled a little sadly. 'Oh love, come on. He's off the table. I'm not saying that to hurt you, but to be sensible. Because one, he's going to be your boss. And b),' she hiccupped, not noticing her list system had changed. 'You swore off men last year. You told me to keep you away from anyone for 12 months. You signed a piece of paper. Want me to get the photo up? It wasn't my idea. It was yours. After…' she tailed off.

'I know.'

'After Jake.'

'I said I know,' Mia repeated, firmly.

'And the way he treated you,' Ellie finished.

'I know.'

The two women sat in silence with only the sounds of Harry Styles' *As It Was* tinkling from the piano to break it and Mia watched a couple a few booths away. They were roughly her age, and whilst she looked on she saw the man lean over and gently kiss his girlfriend on the lips. He then said something which made them both laugh together. They were in their own private bubble, unaware of anyone else in the over decorated bar and Mia sighed, realising just how much she missed having someone she could have that sense of togetherness with.

'I'm sorry.' Ellie spoke marginally first, with Mia tailing a little behind with her own apology. 'But you told me to stop you from getting your heart broken again.'

She put her arm out for Mia who leant in on her friend's shoulder, resting her head to halt the world from spinning. Both women were remembering the period of darkness after Jake, Mia's boyfriend for two years, had left her with no apology or explanation. Just a note to say he wasn't good enough for her.

In her darkest of days, Mia hadn't seen the point of getting out of bed. She would stare at the ceiling, willing herself to cry, to let the pain out in any way she could. But nothing. From the day he'd left she'd felt nothing. It was as though her heart had been carved out and replaced with a lump of useless stone, barely beating save to keep her on the edges of being alive.

But every day Ellie would arrive at her flat at 4.30am, let herself in and wake Mia with a coffee. Whereupon she'd coax and shove and plead with Mia until she'd managed to get her into a shower, forced her to change into the café uniform that included a red polo t-shirt with *Tiers of Joy* printed on the back, and pushed her out of the flat, into the street where they'd walk to the café.

Once in the café it was as though a different Mia would wake up, her hands knowing what to do even if her brain wasn't cooperating. She would mix and leave dough to rise, and create delicious cakes and buns. She was so detached that by the time she'd decorated and begun to bring the first baked goods through to the café's counter in time for the early birds through the door at 8am, she'd be astonished as to where it had all come from.

It had worked though. Ellie's pushing and prodding. Every day she'd wake Mia. Every day she'd bring her home, make her dinner and leave at 9pm, before repeating it the next day.

Except Mondays. The one and only day they closed the café. On Mondays Mia could spend the whole day uninterrupted, just lying in her bed.

Waiting.

For what, she didn't know. But she wasted weeks doing nothing on Mondays.

Until one day when there was a leaflet left in her flat's post-box, which, owing to its bright yellow paper managed to capture her attention. It had advertised Yoga in the Trees and something in Mia ignited the smallest of flames. The idea of stretching her body in the peace of nature called to her.

So, the following Monday, despite feeling tired and small and weak, she'd arrived at a field on the outskirts of town and felt a smile tug at the edges of her mouth for the first time in weeks. A space amongst a ring of trees had been covered in rugs of many bright colours and patterns. Crystals were hung on branches reflecting the spring sunshine, causing flashes of rainbow coloured light to glance through the trees.

The instructor had beckoned Mia over where she'd chosen a rug decorated in wild multicolour zig-zags. In that hour, where she'd stretched into downwards facing dog, then learnt a sun salutation along with six other women in silence save for the bird song, that's where Mia began to find herself, and peace, once again.

'Mia.' Ellie interrupted her thoughts as she prodded her in the side. 'Are you asleep?'

Feeling torn away from the memory of crystals in trees, Mia jerked awake. 'No, but not far off, I think we should go home,' she replied.

Ellie nodded. 'Good plan, and…sorry again…I didn't mean to suggest he's out of your league. But it's probably not right to work together and be together.'

Mia shook her head. 'No, you're right. I said no men for 12 months and I meant it. It's been 11 months since Jake left and I'm not letting a man affect my work. I'm going to do a great job with this ball and I'm not going to let my heart interfere,' she swallowed down the anger she now felt towards her ex.

Satisfied her friend wasn't in the dark place she'd recovered from, Ellie stood and pulled on her leather jacket, fumbling with the zip through her four martini induced haze.

'Here let me.' Mia helped her friend, zipping her in gently. Ellie swayed a little.

'Thanks.'

Mia held her gaze and realised she'd never thanked Ellie for those months. It was down to her friend that their café, and she, were still standing.

'No, thank *you*. You're the best friend a girl could ask for.' She kissed Ellie gently on the cheek, as a mother would to a child and pulled her in for a hug.

'You won't be saying that tomorrow morning when you're wrestling sourdough starter with a hangover,' Ellie replied, laughing.

Mia joined in. It felt good.

Chapter Four

'A flower wall here and the stage here,' Mia was pointing her ideas out to Will as they walked around the enormous room that was to be the star of the masked ball.

'Stage?'

Mia turned around, surprised Will had spoken. He'd barely said one word as she'd walked him around the room that afternoon, outlining her vision. She'd brought her iPad with her to bring up examples on the screen of how she felt the room could be decorated, and what the food should look like. But he'd waved his hand at her, batting her ideas and her away. And since then, he'd been mute as she'd talked, giving more and more detail, filling his silences with her ideas.

'Yes, a stage. For the band? We agreed a live band would be more enjoyable than some music just played over speakers.' She crossed her fingers, if he started saying no to significant things like the music, she just knew the event wouldn't work. A silence had descended over the enormous room and Mia closed her eyes briefly, imagining the ball as it could be.

'Oh, of course. Sorry, I thought you meant there'd be a show, like a cabaret,' Will replied, patting her on the shoulder and jolting Mia's eyes open to the reality of the currently bare room with its exposed oak flooring and stacks of chairs and tables. The room might be blessed with numerous chandeliers and gilt decorations, but it was going to take a lot to bring her vision to life she acknowledged.

She grinned at Will. 'Cabaret? Erm, no, I don't think so; it's hardly a cruise. Just a six piece band.'

'Just?' He raised an eyebrow at her and Mia tried to quell the flutter in her belly whenever he looked directly at her with his deep blue eyes. She felt like he knew what she was thinking and she blinked rapidly, hoping he wouldn't see what she'd been thinking of ever since waking that morning in the middle of a dream involving him, her, and a tub of Nutella.

She blushed at the memory.

'Yes, *just*. You're lucky – I had been considering a ten piece,' she admitted and he grinned.

Will looked at her properly for what felt like the first time that morning as they began walking slowly towards the double doors at the end of the room. 'This is all sounding great and you'll be pleased to know we've already sold the first tickets,' he said as they walked out of the doors and into the long hallway of the manor where every other light was turned off in a bid to save money. It gave the space a gloomy, unloved feel.

'Really? People are actually paying to come?' Mia's stomach flipped again, but this time with nerves.

Will took them into the small kitchen, a space that would have been the servants' quarters when the manor had been built in the 1800s and flicked the kettle on, indicating Mia should take a seat. 'I should hope so, that *is* the point of the event,' he reminded her, his tone returning to steely once again.

'Yes, of course.' Mia didn't know how to explain that whilst she'd organised events before, it had only been within a team where she'd been told what to do and it had been a few years ago. She was starting to worry she'd bitten off too much and she wouldn't be able to pull it off.

Yet again it seemed Will knew what she was thinking. He pressed a cup of hot tea into her hands and sat down opposite her at the beaten up wooden table that would have been more at home in a farmhouse, then smiled at her. 'I chose you for a reason Mia. It's going to be fine,' he said, drinking from his chipped mug which claimed World's Best Grandad.

A question dangled in Mia's mind. She wanted to ask it, but in doing so she'd be opening a can of worms. However, as they sat at the table, their hands wrapped around their mugs in total silence she felt she had to.

'Why *did* you choose me? There are plenty of people with events experience; far more than me. I've only worked as a baker for the past few years. You know as well as I do that my events days are a little behind me,' she said, feeling relieved to have admitted it, though sad it might spell the end for her overseeing the ball. She had such grand plans for it.

Mia was shocked when Will started guffawing, then coughing and indicating his back. Mia leapt to his side, rubbing and patting his back, which she couldn't help but notice was taut with sinewy muscles. After a while, his breathing under control, Will shook his head. 'I am but a lowly cake maker,' he laughed.

Mia was embarrassed. 'I didn't say it like that,' she stuttered, holding tightly onto the mug hoping it would anchor her to the table and stop her from fleeing the awkward situation.

Holding his hands up and smiling broadly, Will sounded apologetic when he spoke. 'I am sorry, but it did sound very self-indulgent and sad. In any case, you asked me why I chose you; it's because of your passion. My friend told me about your wonderful cakes and your ability to conjure something remarkable with them and on the day I was thinking about whether I should approach you, there you were. You and that red Mini, and I thought, yes, perfect.' His eyes were sparkling in the low light and Mia felt her insides squeeze again.

'Who's your friend? I should thank him,' she said, trying to distract herself from how near they were. How much she just wanted to lean towards him and kiss him.

'There you are,' a woman wearing a dark green Barbour jacket with two black Labradors by her side and a scruffy blue beanie hat squashed down over her head, had appeared in the doorway of the kitchen. Her features were hard to make out, owing to the gloomy light, but her voice was filled with plums. Mia squirmed. Women like that regularly made her feel uncomfortable. Inadequate. As though her own state education was something to be ashamed of because she didn't have Eton or Oxford on her CV.

'Who's this young thing?' The woman had her head on one side, sizing Mia up. Noting Will had somehow shifted some distance from her, Mia inhaled and wished for some courage. Standing up and making her way to the woman with her hand extended, she drew herself up to the fullest her 5ft 5in height would allow.

'I'm Mia; Will asked me to organise the masked ball for Valentine's Day. I run the bakery in town, *Tiers of Joy,*' she added by way of explanation, then stopped as a stony silence emanated from the woman who stepped from within the shadow of the doorway so that her features were fully visible. Mia noted she was in her late sixties but with the dewy skin that spoke of many generations of good breeding. And Botox. Her eyes were the duplicate of Will's.

'I am Alicia, William's mother,' she put the emphasis on his full name and Mia winced. 'And I am wondering why he is still forging ahead with this *ghastly* idea when I expressly forbade it. I see no point in allowing riffraff to come traipsing through, ruining our home.'

Mia looked in Will's direction, speechless and caught off guard.

'Mother,' Will stood up and made his way to both women, 'as I've told you before, the council ran this place into the ground. Now we own it, I want it to pay for itself. It'll cost a fortune to run if we don't open it up and use it for events. You know this,' he said, placing a hand on his mum's shoulder to calm her.

'But it's my home.'

Will sighed. 'It'll remain that way; we won't be opening up all of it.'

'Yes, but I grew up here before Papa decided he'd had enough of country living, sending me off to boarding school whilst they moved to Mayfair,' his mother replied quickly. 'This is our chance to enjoy the building again.'

Mia watched the interaction between the two, wondering who the mysterious grandfather was that had gifted his daughter an enormous country house. One which came with so many lightbulbs to replace and countless wonky roof tiles, she wasn't sure it if was a blessing or a curse for them.

Alicia stared at Mia, eyeing her up and down and finally spoke.

'I don't like this idea. Not one bit. I'll hold you entirely responsible *Mia* when it all goes, inevitably, wrong.'

At that, she turned on her heel, the dogs in tow and left Mia and Will in stunned silence.

Chapter Five

'Bloody notes. Honestly Mia, you're going to have to do something with these.' Ellie stuffed the pink notelets she'd found shoved in the back of the pantry amongst the many flours and sugars, into Mia's hands. 'I can't keep finding them.'

Mia accepted the bundle and placed them on the windowsill, making a mental note to bring them home.

'I just miss him, that's all.'

Ellie came over to where Mia was sat on one of two wooden barstools in the kitchen, tears threatening at the corners of her eyes and indicated the pot of strawberry goo currently bubbling on the stove. 'I miss him too. But he'd want you to move on; he wouldn't want tears in the jam.'

Mia smiled weakly. 'I know. But we'd grown so close; I was very fond of him.'

Ellie poked her lightly in the ribs. 'That's because he tipped so well.'

'That's an awful thing to say,' Mia said, hurt on behalf of Albert's feelings. Albert was a frail, elderly man who had been their first customer through their doors when they'd opened. He'd peered into their empty café which they'd decorated in balloons of every colour imaginable, and smiled in delight.

'It's my birthday today, did you do this for me?' he'd asked, with what Mia came to discover was his usual wry humour. Mia had asked him which seat was to become his – he chose a big squashy leather armchair which faced out on to the pedestrianised street out front, so he could watch the world go by. She'd then asked him what he wanted, but instead of ordering, he'd encouraged her to choose on his behalf. His only stipulation being no carrot cake – he hated the vegetable apparently.

And that's how the next year or so played out.

Albert would visit their café five mornings a week, would always sit in what became known by the regulars as 'Albert's seat' and would never order, relying on Mia to choose the appropriate hot drink and sweet morsel for him. He'd try everything she gave him, exclaiming over the delicate piping on a piece of cake, or the flood icing on a special biscuit.

He'd ask her questions about recipes but on most occasions he would sit, staring outside, watching the world go by. After an hour he would slowly make his way out and always, from the first day to his last visit, he would leave a pink note tucked under the saucer with something cheerful written on it for Mia. Along with a tip that was worth twice what the products ever were. She'd told him in the early days he was overpaying, but the answer he gave, his rheumy eyes fixed on hers was, 'there's no price I wouldn't pay for this company'.

Then one day his visits stopped.

Although Ellie and Mia scoured the obituaries for him, they realised they'd only ever known him as Albert, and had no idea where he lived, or what his surname was. But they'd assumed the worst. He had, by his own admission, 'passed 90 some time ago' and had been in poor health the month before.

So now all that was left was a year's worth of pink notes and a sign that said 'Albert's Seat' on it, that a regular had made.

Which was why when Mia had found a pink note left by the cake up at Shawford Manor, she'd been surprised but thrilled that Albert seemed to be alive. Not just that, he was leaving her notes again.

'I found another one.' She said to Ellie as they decanted the jam into jars. Some would be sold in the café, others would be used in fillings for their cakes.

'Another what?' Ellie was attempting to screw the lids onto the very hot glass jars, wincing as she did so.

'An Albert note.' Mia said, smiling. 'There, all done.' The two began to pack the industrial dishwasher.

Ellie looked at her oddly. 'Are you sure? I thought he'd…you know…' She made her eyebrows bounce upwards a little. 'Gone up there.'

Mia shrugged. 'Me too, but maybe we were wrong? I definitely found a note.' She looked in her rucksack that had seen better days and found the note. She handed it to Ellie triumphantly.'

'When life gives you lemons, make lemon icing,' Ellie read it then looked at Mia with a heavy degree of confusion etched across her face. 'Err, what?'

Mia took the note off her and laughed. 'It's nonsense, isn't it; but Albert would regularly leave silly phrases as well as compliments. So it's not an odd thing for him to say.'

'If you're sure,' Ellie seemed sceptical and Mia could understand it. But if it wasn't Albert leaving notes; albeit mysteriously and only up at Shawford Manor, who else could it be?

'Are you ladies free to help out? It's getting busy out here,' Sam appeared around the doorway of the kitchen briefly and Mia gave her a quick nod, grinning at Ellie as their assistant disappeared whilst yelling, 'I'm coming.'

Ellie looked concerned. 'We better get out there or she'll have scared all our customers away.'

'I'll just finish this and be right with you,' Mia said, screwing the last of the jam jar lids on. Satisfied at a job well done she wiped her hands on a cloth and glanced at the note she'd left on the counter. Whatever Ellie thought Mia was certain it was from Albert. Though she did recognise it was odd he'd begun sending them after a three month break, and he'd not made an appearance at the café.

Just as she was going out to help the others her phone began to ring. Seeing it was Will, she answered the call.

'Mia, did you organise for a journalist to be here? He's asking for you; seems to know a lot about the masked ball?' Will's voice was filled with concern and Mia's stomach dropped. In the flurry of activity surrounding the ball this past week, she'd forgotten to let Will know.

'I'm so sorry, yes. But he's early. He wasn't due until 10 o clock,' she remembered, looking at the clock in the kitchen. The digital numbers definitely said 8.45am.

'Well, he's here now,' Will said, all trace of the calm man she'd encountered disappearing. 'What do I say? Can you get up here?' Mia hesitated, she needed to help Ellie and Sam with the café and she could hear how busy things were. But if she didn't run the masked ball, the earnings of which they needed, soon there wouldn't be any customers.

'Mia?'

'Okay, yes. I'm coming. Stall him.'

'How?'

'I don't know; get your dog to do some tricks,' she replied flippantly, ending the call. She took her apron off and grabbed her bag ready to dash out, then stopped for a moment with a thought. She placed a jar of jam and four of her signature cinnamon buns into the bag too. Popping her head round the door to what was definitely a busy morning scrum, Mia called over to Ellie.

'I'm so sorry; emergency up at the manor. I'll be back as soon as possible.'

Ellie pressed the lid on two coffees, handing it to a customer in overalls and nodded. 'We've got this under control, go.'

'I'll be back soon, I promise.'

Mia dashed out of the door knowing that she and Ellie needed a proper conversation soon. The prices of everything were going up, people weren't spending as much and the café was haemorrhaging money. Even busy mornings weren't going to be enough to keep them going. Sooner rather than later, she and Ellie were going to have to make some tough decisions about their baby business. She knew it had been a dream of Ellie's to run a café, and it had been a perfect way for Mia to bake for a living. But it didn't matter how friendly the two were, if the numbers weren't working they needed to figure out next steps. Mia knew Ellie would be aware, but maybe as it was her idea she was burying her head in the sand.

Filing her worries to the back of her mind for the time being, she jumped into Rose and breathed a sigh of relief when the car started first time. Despite the usual roadworks attempting to slow her down, Mia pulled up onto the long drive within 15 minutes of Will's call. He was stood in the doorway to the hall with another man who Mia assumed had to be the journalist. Both of whom were watching Digby the Labrador rolling over.

'Hi,' Mia extended her hand to the journalist. 'I'm...'

'This is Mia, she's the organiser of the event.' Will said quickly. 'Heel'. The last word was something Mia wasn't expecting and she almost did as she was told, until she realised it was directed at Digby, who stopped his performance and sat happily next to his master's leg. 'That's enough of that I think,' he said. 'Mia, this is Alex, from the *Mistlebrook Gazette*.'

Mia extended a hand to the man in his mid-20s, who looked in need of a haircut and an iron. She could see his creased shirt peeking through his dark green anorak and smiled. She had friends who worked in local journalism and respected the career which was being rapidly removed owing to AI apps and bloggers.

'Hi Alex, sorry I'm late,' she said, grinning at the man who smiled back.

'No, I'm sorry, it turns out I got the wrong time. But I've been kept entertained by the man of the manor, though he doesn't seem all that keen to be interviewed.' Mia looked at Will who had the decency to at least look a touch embarrassed.

'Not really my area,' Will said, smiling. 'I make a good cup of tea though. How about I do that whilst Mia talks you through the plan?' Alex nodded and they watched as Will made his way into the country house.

'Right, shall we?' Alex asked, as Mia smiled, wondering where to start. 'Can you tell me a little more about this masked ball? Do you mind if I record you? It helps with writing it up, plus I can put a short video about it up on our socials,' he explained, holding up his phone. Mia cursed herself for not checking in a mirror before leaving the café, but she'd been in a rush and hadn't realised she'd be on camera.

'Sure. But just be kind, I've been up since 4am baking,' she said, smiling. 'I might have a bit of flour here and there.'

Alex looked confused. 'Baking? But I thought you were an event organiser?'

Mia smiled warmly. 'I am. I'm both. I used to be an event organiser for a full time job, but then I made my dream come true and set up a café and bakery with my best friend. Happily I've had a chance to organise this event too,' she explained, 'I brought you a little something by the way,' she remembered and handed the bag of baked goods and jam to Alex who looked in the bag and beamed.

'That's really kind. These smell incredible; I hope you're not trying to bribe me?'

Mia laughed. 'No, I don't think jam really counts. I just thought you'd enjoy them.'

Alex nodded. 'Thank you. I've got a busy day ahead, this will keep me going I'm sure. Shall we get on with the interview?'

This time it was Mia's turn to nod. 'Go for it.' There was a chill in the air as they stood on the steps, and Mia hoped they be able to get inside quickly.

'Do you know Mr Monroe?' Alex asked.

'No, why?'

Putting his phone down, Alex looked at Mia with confusion. 'Sorry, I don't think I understand. If you used to be an event organiser but aren't any more, and you don't know Will all that well, how did it come about that he asked you to organise his ball? It's quite a big ask for someone who doesn't do it professionally anymore. Isn't it?'

Mia considered her response carefully. Everything the journalist was saying was what she'd thought too, but she'd chosen to assume someone had recommended her to Will. Though it was odd. Especially when he could have kept on one of the events planners who'd been working at the house until recently.

'Mia?' Alex prompted.

She shook her head and plastered on a smile. 'You know how it is. Small town. We all recommend each other. Let's go into the house.'

Chapter Six

Mia tried to empty her thoughts of the awful interview as she lay amongst the trees, breathing in the oxygen. It was freezing in the woods but Gloria, the yoga teacher, believed in year-round practice. They'd so far performed their downward dogs and goddess squats in everything from a blizzard, to torrential rain, to burning heat. In fact the only time Mia had known it be cancelled was when there had been a risk of lightning and trees acting as conductors had been a step too far. Even for Gloria.

Gloria spoke from the stool she sat on, covered in a spotted blanket, looking very similar to a toadstool as far as Mia was concerned. 'Exhale, get rid of the stale air at the bottom of your lungs and send it upwards.'

She tried to focus on her breathing. In – Will did nothing to help. Out – Alex really twisted her words. In – Will should have been there answering. Out – so what if she forgot the main things she wanted to talk about in the interview? She'd managed to get one line in about the masked ball, which was something.

In fact, she thought, as she got into the cat position and started pushing through. Really Will could have told her a lot more about the hall's history and how he came to be custodian *before* the article came out. Rather than her finding out in the paper on a Saturday morning when a regular to the café drew her attention to it.

'He inherited it from Albert?' She'd read in shock that Will's grandfather was William Bertrand Randolph Walters. Known by his pals as Albert. Neither she nor Ellie had known that was his name when they'd been scouring the obituaries for the last few months. Mia was devastated to have missed the funeral but more so, she was annoyed Will hadn't told her.

'Mia, we're about to begin our sun salutations. Are you joining us?' Gloria spoke quietly. Not expecting nor chastising, she never forced anyone to go into a position they didn't want to do. But she did offer suggestions when she thought they may need it.

Looking around her, Mia realised she was the only person still in cat pose, whereas everyone else was standing.

'Sorry Gloria,' she said quietly but the yoga teacher shook her head.

'We have nothing to apologise for. If we need more space to sit, we can. If we need to stretch, we will. If we need to scream or cry, it's allowed. There is no right way. Just your own.'

'Okay, sorry,' said Mia, catching herself, then grinning. She decided to focus entirely on her yoga session, with no thoughts to newspaper articles.

Later that morning however when she was back home, Mia was trying to look up money making ideas for the café by researching what other businesses were doing when Will called. She sighed. She'd ignored his calls ever since the article came out. But she needed to talk to him about the event if nothing else.

'Yes?' she answered, picking up the phone and mustering every ounce of sincerity she could.

'You saw it then?' Will said, with no preamble. 'Look, I said I didn't like journalists, but you insisted.'

Mia shook her head. 'I stand by it. We need the publicity. The event is just a few weeks away. We're asking quite a lot to sell it out in such a short time without telling anyone about it.'

'Point taken, but I don't know why they've had to dig up everything about my family,' Will replied.

Looking at a small statue of a Buddha she'd picked up in a charity shop the day before and hoping it would imbue some sense of calm in her before she replied, Mia inhaled. 'They didn't dig anything up. It was a story; they were informing readers that a beautiful country house that used to be owned by an eccentric billionaire, which had been given to a council has reverted to his grandson. Bypassing his own daughter. It sounds like a news story to me.'

'Multi-millionaire. He wasn't a billionaire. Plus I'm not sure if he was eccentric, just moody,' Will corrected.

Mia frowned. 'That's not how I remember him.'

There was a silence on the end of the phone. 'You knew my grandfather?'

Looking towards her window, where a peace lily that needed more love and attention than she remembered to give it wilted, Mia smiled a little sadly. 'I did. He used to visit us most mornings.'

'Us?' Will sounded very confused. Mia stood and stretched her back.

'Yes, *us*. He used to come to the café every weekday. I used to make him something different every day. He'd spend an hour or so with us. Then he'd go.' She was quiet for a moment. 'I hadn't realised he'd passed away though. I was sorry to hear it. He meant a lot.'

'Did he?' Will sounded incredulous.

'Well, yes. He was a lovely old man, we had a lot of fun with him.'

'That's not how I remember Gramps. He rarely spoke a word to me and when he did it was usually about how disappointed he was. Mum said that from the day her mum left Gramps stopped being happy. That was 30 years ago, and I'm not sure I saw him smile in all that time,' Will said quietly, his voice on the phone sounded sad yet sincere.

Mia was shocked. 'I wonder if I'm mixed up. Albert would laugh along with us, he'd tell us jokes…'

'Tell you jokes? I can't think it was him then. I don't think Gramps knew even one joke. Let alone *jokes,* plural,' Will spluttered.

Remembering the laughter that had rung out around the café when Albert was in there Mia shook her head. 'I must be making a mistake. Maybe we need to think about something else. How are the sales going?'

'We've sold about half the tickets so far, and there's only three weeks to go.'

Mia could hear the concern in Will's voice and willed herself to sound steelier than she was. 'It's fine, it's all going to be okay.'

'You sound as certain as I feel,' he said, laughing. 'Are you doing anything today? I've been invited somewhere; want to join me?'

Looking around, aware she only had one day a week to spend on herself, the flat, her ironing, and the various plans for the masked ball. Mia knew she should say no.

'It involves chocolate,' Will added.

With zero hesitation, Mia replied, 'I'm in.' She pressed end after they'd agreed he'd be along in half an hour, which gave her just enough time to get changed from her yoga gear and pull the twigs out of her hair; one of the issues with outdoors exercise. Mia paused by her dressing table and pondered putting make-up on. Then changed her mind. She only wore it when she was going out for the evening. Or she was on a date. As it was a grey, late January afternoon and she was going out with her boss this definitely wasn't a date.

She picked up a light pink lip-gloss and brushed it on. It couldn't hurt to look a *little* smarter than usual. Just for her sake of course.

Mia threw her keys into her tiny black rucksack along with her phone, then pulled on some trainers. She locked the door to her flat and made her way out into the street, whilst fighting with her very warm, but awkward to put on, wool lined coat. It was a bright cherry red and kept her super warm, but was a tiny bit snug across the shoulders; something not helped by wearing a bulky jumper underneath and always required a bit of a wiggle to get it on. Just as she was walking round the corner, where she was due to meet Will, she walked straight into someone.

'Look where you're going. I'm carrying a coffee, I could have been...' The voice attached to the body spoke gruffly then broke off. 'Oh, hey Mia. Sorry. I didn't mean to snap,' Liam coloured a little.

Mia was close to asking what the difference was between then and all the other times he'd been rude to her in the café, but decided to keep her words in check.

'I think it was fairly even, I walked into you; you walked into me. If anything, I should be the one complaining,' she smiled, trying to sound light-hearted. 'You could have sent me flying.' The hours spent working in his father's greengrocers lifting heavy products and dealing with deliveries meant he was strong and toned. And very solid from what Mia had just walked into.

He laughed a little uncomfortably and ran a hand through his light brown hair. 'That's a good point; sorry again.' He looked at her, then looked at her, as though trying to work something out.

'What?'

'You look...different,' was all he managed before a car beeped and Mia looked over to see Will had pulled up on the road opposite in his beaten up Land Rover.

Mia flushed a little with embarrassment and tried to cover it with a breezy manner. 'It's just because you haven't seen me out of my apron. This is what a baker looks like in the wild. Have a good day Liam,' she said, laughing, then headed over to the car and pulled let herself into the passenger side.

The warmth of the heater Will had on full blast was a welcome respite from the chill outside and she moved her hands over it.

Mia saw Liam on the other side of the road. He'd not moved from where she'd walked into him. Instead he was sipping his coffee, browsing the window of the antique shop she liked to look in. The back of his head to them. That was the first time they'd had a conversation where he hadn't just grunted his hello at her. He seemed to save his pleasantries for Ellie.

'Shall we?' Will said, smiling at her warmly. Mia tried to ignore the flutter of butterflies in her stomach at the way he looked at her.

'Sure; and that would be where?'

He patted his finger to his nose, conspiratorially. 'All will become clear soon enough,' he said, revving the engine and pulling out into the road.

Chapter Seven

'I didn't know this place existed.' Mia's eyes widened at the sight of the chocolate factory in front of her. She unclipped her seatbelt and sat in the warmth of the car, looking at the warehouse they'd parked in front of. Looking over at her, Will grinned, then opened his door, the blast of cold air shocking Mia into action.

They'd only been driving for 20 minutes. Being from the area for so long, Mia was certain she knew the district like the back of her hand. But when they'd pulled into the unassuming industrial estate with a carpet manufacturer on one side, a garage on the other and then, round a corner the warehouse they were coming to visit. She was utterly surprised, especially as the warehouse was covered in sky blue boarding with a vivid pink logo on the front announcing *Cocoa Couture*.

'Shall we?' Will had appeared at her side of the car and was offering his hand to help her down. Smiling at the old-fashioned nature of it, Mia accepted. His hand was warm and a little bit rough as though he'd spent the morning chopping wood. Which, she pondered for a moment, he may well have done. She didn't know anything about what he did when he wasn't organising a masked ball, or turning up at her café. She reluctantly let go of his hand, reminding herself of the vow she'd taken to avoid all relationships for a year. She hadn't just spent the last 12 months getting over one man to entangle herself with another. Will didn't seem to notice. Instead he was grinning at the building. 'It's pretty striking, isn't it?' Mia said. 'I love the colour combination.'

'I love the smell,' Will said, sniffing enthusiastically. 'Come on, I want some chocolate.' She laughed at his excitement and followed him to the building.

Introducing themselves to the receptionist, who was sat surrounded by empty sky blue boxes, all needing to be packed with pink shredded paper before the chocolates were added, they were told to wait for the owner to come.

'Is Willy Wonka going to come out?' Mia asked quietly, causing Will to smile.

'I hope so, I think oompa loompas might be a bit out of date now though,' he whispered back and Mia grinned.

'I don't know, they could give some celebrities a run for their money with the bright orange tans.'

Both were giggling when someone with peroxide blonde hair and a jumpsuit that had patterns in every colour backed out of the factory still talking to an unseen person through the door.

'No, I think more coconut.'

The owner of the jumpsuit turned around and their face split into an enormous smile.

'You must be Will; and you're the café lady.' The two were engulfed in a tight hug, then released.

'I am; he is, but how do you know who we are?' Mia replied, thrilled with the joy that seemed to emanate from the owner.

'Easy, I saw your article in the *Mistlebrook Gazette*, and I would recognise this chap's intense eyes anywhere.'

Mia laughed at the description. 'Okay, and you are?'

'Me? I'm Lee; I'm the owner of this little land of cocoa and sugar and I just had to get you over here. I think we can do something fun together. But first, we need to get that hair under control.' Lee pointed at Mia's curls, making her go red, then grinned. 'Don't worry, we all need to wear protective gear, but then you get to try loads of chocolate. So it's a small price to pay.'

'Did someone say chocolate?' Mia said, grinning.
'Follow me.'

'Better do as they say.' Will said, and indicated Mia should follow Lee through the door.

The room the three entered had a sink on one wall with numerous hand washing instructions on posters, along with various different white doctors' style coats, hanging on the opposite side. Lee handed Mia and Will a coat each then produced disposable hair nets for them to wear. Lee's hand hovered over the box of beard nets whilst they scrutinised Will's stubbly chin. 'Can't really count that as a beard, can we?' Lee said, their head on one side, considering Will. 'As entertaining as it would be to force that on you.'

Lee walked ahead, as Mia wrestled her hair into her net and did up her coat, feeling both formal and ridiculous at the same time.

Once finished she looked up at Will, took one glance, and snort laughed.

'Now hang on a minute; you're hardly in a position to laugh. Have you seen yourself?' he asked, grinning. But Mia just shook her head. Will's hair net had gathered around his dark hair and made him look a little bit like an alien. Combined with the formality of the lab coat, which covered his signature beaten-up jeans, it was not a look Mia was used to on him.

'Okay, you two. You both look ridiculous, that's kind of the point,' Lee said, popping their head in to see how the two were doing. 'Are you coming?'

As the three walked into the heart of the factory Mia gasped. The scent of melted chocolate permeated the air and everywhere she looked Lee's staff were working on different confections.

'Come over here,' Lee shouted over the noisy machinery, taking them to where a woman was carefully removing multiple chocolate hearts from a mould. They were shiny and looked stunning, but too beautiful to eat. 'We're at our second busiest point in the calendar, Christmas is the busiest of course, but coming up to Valentine's we sell *a lot* of chocolate.' Lee gave them each a heart. Mia popped hers in whole and was enthralled with the creaminess of the dark chocolate that was cut through by a delicious caramel that had just the slightest tang of salt in it.

'That's incredible,' she said, savouring it.

Lee continued showing them around to each chocolatier who was weaving their cocoa magic to create delectable truffles, gorgeous fudges and some incredibly shiny dark chocolate and raspberry caramels that looked as though they'd been dipped in gold. Mia's brain was in overdrive as she thought how she could incorporate the chocolates in her bakes.

'This way for coffee and chocolate, if you've got the stomach for any more of course,' Lee said, grinning as they opened a door to a cosy office, that was the epitome of calm as the factory noise disappeared.

Will grinned at Mia. 'You're beaming, I knew you'd love it here.'

'I'm just glad you took up my offer of a visit.' Lee said, making them coffees from a pod machine. 'These won't be up to your level I'm afraid, but it'll have to do.'

'Have you been to my café? I would have thought I'd recognise you, I've got a good memory for faces,' she said.

Lee shook their head. 'No, but I've heard very good things. A lot of my staff go to you for their coffees and whatnots on their days off. I hear your cinnamon buns are the stuff of dreams. Two awards isn't it?'

Mia blushed. 'We do our best.'

'Not to take the light away from Mia,' Will said, accepting his mug of coffee. 'But you did invite us here with an idea in mind I think? Not just the incredible tour of course,' he added hastily, though Mia could tell Will was keen to get to the business aspect of the afternoon.

Lee sat back and sipped some coffee. 'Of course. I have a proposition for you, but it would involve the two of you.'

Will and Mia looked at each other and shrugged.

'Okay?' Mia prompted.

'I would like to open a chocolate café. But it's more than that. I want a place where people can make them, can learn about them, can buy them of course too, but somewhere where the passion of this place can be distilled into a café space. I would like to open it at your manor, Will, and I'd like you to oversee the running of it.'

There was a silence in the room.

'I thought you were suggesting something with the masked ball?' Will said.

Lee smiled. 'Well of course, I said to you I'd happily provide favours for your ball. I think mini masks would be divine, and I'd do them for free.'

'That's amazing. Really?' Mia clasped her hands together with joy.

'Of course, but only if we're in agreement of the chocolate café going in, we'd be business partners essentially, so I'd be more than happy to throw a few free chocolates your way,' Lee explained patiently.

Mia looked at Will, willing him to say something but he was staying quiet.

'It's a very kind offer, but I'm not sure,' she said quietly. 'I have my own café. I don't know how I could run another. Plus with the ball and everything it's quite busy already.'

Lee nodded. 'I completely understand, but I think you misunderstand. I don't expect you to run two cafes, I would want you just to run the chocolate one.' Seeing her hesitation Lee rushed on. 'Don't you see what a golden opportunity this would be for you? For the both of you? The manor is perfect for weddings, even if the council did everything they could to run it into the ground. Once it's done up again, you'll have brides and grooms desperate to have their weddings there. With all the work you're doing on the masked ball it will become the destination place for events in the area too. We could become a one-stop wedding and events shop. My chocolates as favours, your cakes for the weddings. We could even offer chocolate themed hen and stag nights.'

'But a café? Isn't that a bit...' Will tailed off.

'It's not a bit anything. Think of all the National Trust places with restaurants and cafés and they all cope with weddings and events in their properties. Anyway, it wouldn't be any old café, it would be a destination one. Somewhere where people want to be photographed.'

'I see,' said Will, sipping his coffee thoughtfully. 'It's a very good idea. Do you have a business plan?'

Mia watched the two in horror as Lee handed a pile of documents to Will. 'Of course. All costings, my offer, my share – all the boring stuff – all in there. All you two have to do is say yes.'

'Can we think on it?' Mia asked, worried Will might sign on the dotted line there and then.

Lee smiled. 'I wouldn't have it any other way.'

A little later as they left, Mia waved at Lee but moved Will briskly along to the car. Once inside, she turned to him to say what had been on her mind since the proposal, but he spoke at the same time.

'How do we get out of that then?'

'That's something to think about.'

'What?'

Chapter Eight

'You can't honestly think I'll give up my business for someone else's? You know why Lee's asking me to manage it, don't you?' Mia was angry at Will's lack of understanding.

Will shook his head.

'Because that way it's one less café in competition. It makes good business sense. But I'm not turning my back on Ellie. Or the regulars,' she said, sadly.

'It's a huge opportunity though,' Will said firmly, as he negotiated the car out of the trading estate and back out onto the country road.

'For you maybe.'

Will turned to look at her briefly. 'I think you need to talk to Ellie. See what she has to say. Haven't you spent the last few weeks complaining to me about how much work it is to keep your café going?'

Mia widened her eyes in shock. 'I have not, as you said, "complained for the past few weeks". I've just shared with a friend my concerns. But clearly I was mistaken, you're just looking out for what's best for you.' A silence crept into the car.

As they drove past hedgerows, sending birds flying upwards, Mia watched a magpie take off. 'One for sorrow,' she said, absentmindedly.

'What's that?' Will's tone was harsh, and Mia willed the journey to be over sooner rather than later.

'Nothing.'

'You said one for sorrow.' Will looked at her briefly. 'Didn't you?'

Mia shrugged. 'So?'

'Nothing, it's just...it's something my granddad used to say.'

The quiet enveloped them both again.

Mia spoke quietly. 'Albert used to say those sorts of things, so it's stuck with me. But it's a pretty common saying.'

'This Albert guy meant a lot to you?'

'Yes, he was very sweet.'

Will shook his head. 'Definitely not my grandfather. No-one could accuse him of being sweet.'

'You know, we could settle this. Do you have a photo of your granddad?' Mia asked as they swung into her road and she exhaled in relief that the awkward drive was coming to an end.

'Of course, but it's from about ten years ago. The last time I saw him. I'll bring it to the café tomorrow,' Will said.

'We have one of him from a few months ago, he was part of our one-year anniversary celebrations,' Mia said, remembering the event fondly.

'Okay; it's a deal.'

Mia got out of the car and was just about to swing the door shut, when Will called something out.

'What was that?' She reopened the door watching as he chewed his lip, clearly unsure whether to repeat himself or not.

'Just that, maybe we can talk about future plans tomorrow?'

Mia shook her head. 'I think I'll need longer to decide than that. I'm going to have to talk to Ellie to begin with. I'm not having her thinking I'm leaving her in the lurch.'

Something crossed Will's face, quickly replaced with a big smile. 'Of course. You wouldn't want to do that. Don't forget your bag,' he said, handing her the backpack she brought everywhere.

'Thanks, bye.'

As she made her way to the flat, Mia couldn't help shake the feeling she was missing something, but as she replayed the conversations with Will and Lee she couldn't put a finger on what it was. Shaking her head at the fact she'd been too preoccupied with the making of chocolate, she stopped to collect the mail from her letterbox and made her way upstairs to her flat.

Mia opened the door and flung the letters and bag down on her counter, turning to fill the kettle, and find a mug and teabag. She turned back, catching her bag and the letters, and knocked them all to the floor. 'Damn,' she said, as she picked up the detritus that had spilled on the floor including scraps of paper with recipe ideas on, and a very large collection of receipts she needed to give to her accountant. The post had scattered across the floor too, mainly junk mail promoting pizza delivery and cleaning services.

But it was the pink paper which attracted Mia's attention. A small slip of heart shaped paper, peeking out from under her bag. She pulled at it and smiled. It had one word on it.

Sorry x

Grinning slightly, Mia's heart began to thud a little. Will *was* sweet on her. She knew it. He'd been behaving like a gentleman, other than their mini fight earlier. He hadn't tried to pursue a relationship whilst they were working together. But he'd given himself away. He'd slipped an apology into her bag, then made sure she had it back.

It made sense as well. The other note, which had been left up at the manor those weeks ago, was when she first ran into him.

He'd said he was coming to the café tomorrow. With a photo of Albert to compare against hers – but of course it would be the same man. Albert would have told Will about the notes at some point, and, when the old man had passed, Will had decided the way to get her attention, and her heart, was to mimic them.

It was quite sweet really, she thought, as she stirred her tea. He must have known Albert a lot better than he was letting on.

'What am I thinking?' she said out loud to the peace lily. 'I'm sworn off men.' The plant didn't give her much of response. Instead, she took her tea and sat down on the worn red sofa in her living room and curled her legs under her, wondering whether swearing off someone like Will was a good idea. He was, in her mum's terms, "a bit of a catch". Handsome. Kind. Thoughtful. He was a bit grouchy, and his mum was a nightmare, but that came with the territory. And she wasn't certain about becoming a lady of the manor. She bit her lip. Not that she was thinking that far ahead of course. She smiled to herself.

Maybe a little bit.

Thinking about the next day and Will coming into the café, she wondered whether she should bring up the note. She didn't want him to think she didn't know. But then, why was he doing it in such a subtle way? Maybe he didn't want to tell her to her face, just yet. Maybe he wanted to get past the masked ball first.

Then there was the issue with the café. She needed to talk to Ellie, but Mia, though tempted by how easy it would be to just say yes to Lee, wasn't keen on ditching their dream and giving up *Tiers of Joy*. It seemed ridiculous to give it up, and for what? To run someone else's business? The more she thought about it, the more certain she was that she wasn't going to say yes.

Will would understand. She knew he would. Especially as he'd shown his intentions towards her. In fact, it wouldn't be sensible to mix romance and business. Much better to keep them separate.

Nodding at her decision, Mia decided to have her favourite kind of night in. A rerun of The Great British Bake Off, followed by an early bedtime, surrounded by her favourite baking cookbooks.

And she definitely wouldn't be thinking about a certain someone with sparkly blue eyes, who would be making a visit to her café again tomorrow.

Definitely not.

Chapter Nine

The next morning however all thoughts of sparkly blue eyes and creative bakes went out of the window when Mia arrived at the bakery at five am, ready to start making bread.

Water was all over the floor of the café. It was deep enough to come up to her ankles and was already making its way ever higher on the sofas, causing irreparable damage.

Her first thought was someone had left a tap running. She dashed behind the counter to have a look but the problem wasn't coming from there. Barging through the fire door into the kitchen she stopped in dismay as water gushed from a cracked pipe that led to their industrial sized dishwasher and was pumping across the floor into the main part of the café.

Looking around in desperation, Mia tried to keep calm and remember what the landlord had told her. There was a lever somewhere which stopped the water coming into the kitchen. Methodically her eyes followed the pipe, down behind the lockers where she remembered the lever was placed, just out of sight. She quickly ran to the red lever and pulled it up hard, noting the groaning of the old pipes disagreeing with her actions. Water still pumped from the pipe, flooding the floor and Mia's jeans were soaked to the knee. Looking around she wondered what her priorities were. There was electrical equipment everywhere, and she knew that meant the chances of her getting electrocuted could be high. Her thoughts were interrupted by a commotion at the front door.

'What the?' Ellie's words disappeared as she looked around the devastation. 'What's happened?'

Mia turned to see her friend, struggling to keep the tears from her eyes. 'Everything's ruined, isn't it?'

'Come on, out.' Ellie pulled Mia from the kitchen, through the café and out onto the street, where dawn hadn't broken and the street lights left pools of orange on the pavement.

'I think I stopped it. I pulled the lever,' Mia said, as she watched Ellie call 999 and explain the situation to the fire brigade. When her friend was finished on the call, she pulled Mia in for a hug.

'It's not looking great. We need to call the landlord. But we're going to be closed for weeks.'

Mia let Ellie call the landlord and tell him what had happened. She watched her friend's face closely, trying to judge if he was blaming them or not. As soon as Ellie got off the phone, she sunk to the floor.

'He's saying he's going to have it investigated but if it's our fault, we could be facing a hefty bill,' she said. 'The insurance won't pay out if it was our fault.'

Mia shook her head. 'But it can't be our fault; the pipe was cracked, I could see that. It's age.'

'True. Though I'm surprised I didn't see it yesterday, a crack that large... water would have started to come through as soon as I put the dishwasher on yesterday.'

'Why did you come in yesterday, we weren't open?' Mia asked suddenly.

Ellie shifted a little, slightly embarrassed. 'You're going to think I'm lame.'

'We're best friends, how could I think that?'

Ellie looked up at the lightening sky. 'I've been trying to improve my bread skills. You're so good, but you have to come in every morning and I've seen the impact the early mornings are taking on you. The toll. I wanted to give you a bit of a break, so we could take it in turns. But I've been practising, trying to get the bread to your level.'

'You do that on your day off?' Mia was shocked her friend had kept such a big secret from her. 'Why didn't you say?'

Ellie shrugged. 'Only for the last month since you've been working on the masked ball. You have so much on, I wanted to help out a bit.' She looked up at Mia. 'I know why you're doing it, you know.'

'What?'

'The ball. It isn't because Will asked you nicely, it's because the cash injection will prop up the café for a bit longer.'

Mia was shocked. 'You knew?'

Ellie smiled and nodded sadly. 'I've not wanted to confront it but things have been getting worse the last few months; it doesn't take a genius to recognise that we're paying more for ingredients, but we're not increasing our own prices. And all the other bills have gone up.'

'Why didn't you say something?' Mia sat down next to her friend.

'Why didn't you?'

Mia's response was washed away when a puddle began leaking through the front door of the café into the street, and with it, she noticed was a pink slip.

'Oh no.' Peering in through the window she could see an army of pink heart shaped notes floating on the water from the kitchen across the café floor. Like a flotilla going into battle.

Mia breathed a small sigh of relief when the lights of an arriving fire engine could be seen reflecting on the buildings towards them. Suddenly the engine appeared with fire persons jumping down and bringing their equipment in to pump the water out. As they opened the door, water washed out of the gap and pink notes, their words smeared away, sped past them down the street.

It was the notes that did it. Every kind word Albert had ever written had disappeared.

Mia leant against the streetlamp and sobbed.

'Here,' Liam had appeared at her side with a thick coat which he put around her shoulders.

'Thank you.' Mia looked at the greengrocer gratefully. She hadn't realised how cold she was until he'd wrapped her up. 'I'm very damp,' she said, shivering. The realisation of what had happened to her business beginning to settle.

'This should help,' Liam offered her a travel cup decorated in a faded panda motif. Mia looked at him in confusion, and he was quick to explain. 'It's an old one of mine I usually have at the shop. It's seen better days, but it has a tea in it. I thought you could use something.'

Mia nodded and sipped, allowing the hot sweet drink do the job it was famous for. 'Thanks Liam, that's really thoughtful,' she said, smiling up at him. She took another sip. 'So, pandas...any reason?' She turned the travel cup around in her hand. It was in fact pink with pandas on it, definitely not what she'd have thought he'd have chosen. He grinned and took it from her.

'If you don't want the brew.'

Mia laughed. 'No, I do...give it back,' she said, gently prising it from his hands and sipping the tea again.

'My sister gave it to me – she's ten years younger than me and thought it would be funny,' he shrugged, talking quietly so Mia had to lean in a little to hear him properly, 'but I just liked that she'd thought of me, so I use it. It makes me smile,' he grinned.

'You never bring it to the café though?' Mia said, remembering as they gave discounts for reusable cups being used.

Liam rolled his eyes. 'Caught I'm afraid. I like to have my coffee in a proper cup in your café,' he coloured a little. 'That is, in the café. It's always nicer than from the plastic cups.'

Mia nodded. 'Not that you'll get the option any time soon.' She grimaced as she watched the water being pumped out of the property. 'I can't believe how much there is.' A man in fire gear who looked officious walked over to them as Ellie appeared at Mia's side.

'So, how bad is it?'

'Are you the owner?' the fireman asked Ellie.

'We run the café,' Mia clarified. 'Though we rent the building.'

The fireman nodded and made a note. 'Okay, well we'll need the details of the owner, it looks like they've not be maintaining the pipes properly. You're lucky this didn't burst when the electrics were on. There could have been a serious problem.'

Mia and Ellie nodded. What they wanted to know was how quickly they could get back in. Liam shifted a little behind Mia and she, for a brief moment, thought how lovely it would be to lean back into him to feel his warmth and support. She immediately brought a stop to her thoughts, only a few hours before she'd been thinking about what it would be like to be with Will. That felt like a lifetime ago.

'How soon can we get in? This afternoon? Tomorrow?' Ellie asked, keen to get things moving.

But the fireman looked at them both in incredulity. 'It'll be months. At least three I'd guess at. I haven't had a full look, but that would be my guess. You'll need to get someone in to assess the damage from the insurance company first. Then you can work on a plan.'

'I think I might...' Mia began, feeling her mind start to go dark and fuzzy, the sign she was going to faint. It hadn't happened for years, only at times of extreme stress. Suddenly the feel of strong arms behind her, holding her up brought her back. Turning, expecting to see Liam, Mia felt an odd sense of confusion as she realised it was Will.

'Hey, you okay?' He held her at arm's length.

'Never better,' she joked, then winced. 'Did I just faint into your arms? How embarrassing.'

'Less embarrassing than whatever you're holding,' Will said, smiling kindly at her at the same time Mia realised she was still clutching Liam's cup. She laughed, handing it back to Liam. 'Thank you for that.' Liam accepted the cup, tucking it into a pocket of his coat and looking away at the café as he did so.

Will looked between the two of them and raised an eyebrow, saying nothing.

'So, what's happened?' he asked, craning his neck around as though he'd be able to see inside the café.

'Flood,' Liam said in a gruff voice. Will looked at him and nodded.

'Got that, thanks; aren't you the guy who supplies the vegetables for our events? Larry isn't it?'

'Liam, but close.'

Will nodded, turning away. 'Okay. See you around.' He rubbed Mia's arms quickly to warm her up, then shifted a touch. 'Who's coat is this? It smells like potatoes,' he said, laughing.

'No need to be rude,' Mia replied, looking to see if Liam had heard. Fortunately the grocer had already moved away though she couldn't be certain he hadn't been party to Will's mocking. Mia had turned to face Will. 'Why are you here? It's very early; no one is here at this sort of time usually.' She looked at her phone, it was barely 6am. The normal sort of time for people like herself, Liam and the butchers to be setting up, but too early for customers. Especially customers like Will who tended to arrive around 10am, after the early morning rush.

Will glanced at Ellie to gauge her reaction to Mia's sharp tone before saying anything. 'I was just in the area, I saw something was going on and thought I'd check. Oh and I brought this.' He rummaged in his pocket.

Mia peered in the gloomy light to see what he was showing her, it was still a long time before sunrise. The photo looked old. A man sat very upright in a stiff wingback chair.

'Who is this?'

Will nodded. 'Thought as much, that's my grandad, looks like this isn't your Albert,' he raised his eyebrows at her.

'Though that makes more sense. Mine was a right grumpy arse, yours sounds much nicer.'

Ellie and Mia re-examined the photo but they had to agree, it wasn't their Albert. Which left the mystery of the old man and the pink notes for Mia to consider on another day. Conscious of all the work they'd need to do to get the café back on its feet, Mia nodded, afraid if she said anything she'd cry.

Another thought came to mind as well, how was she going to juggle working on the masked ball and fixing the café? It had already been a difficult balancing act, now it would be almost impossible.

'I think we should go in and see what's salvageable,' Ellie said, breaking her thoughts. 'We'll figure out our next steps once we've done that. See you around Will,' she said, smiling. Then walked off in the direction of the café, pushing through the throng of rubberneckers who'd settled around the cordon.

'I better go in too, I can't leave Ellie to this by herself,' Mia said, moving away from Will.

He nodded. 'Of course; but I'm here, anything you need. Just say.'

She smiled, relieved to have him as a friend.

'You go back to the manor, I'll be fine.' She tried to think of a way to say she didn't want to think about Lee's offer just yet, or even the ball, but couldn't get her brain to work.

Will caught her wrist in his hand and held it lightly. 'I told you, don't worry, let's just leave it all for now and catch up in a couple of days. Once you've chatted to Ellie. Two days won't harm anything,' he added and smiled.

Mia watched him walk away and took a deep breath before heading into her café. Two days. Two days to decide whether she wanted to ditch everything to do with her café, which, right now was looking very appealing. Or stay and risk losing Will, any chances of events planning, and a lucrative job.

She shook her head. Her focus today was the café. The rest of it would have to wait.

Chapter Ten

'Coffee machine, toaster, sandwich grill. Not the till as the plug shorted, though we might be able to get it fixed.' Ellie listed the items that, because they'd been above the counters had missed getting damaged; though a lot of items had been sprayed by a fireperson who had not been careful when removing the last of the pipes that had sucked up the floodwater.

Two days after the flood, the women were in what remained of their café, still trying to work out what to salvage.

'Most of the cutlery, crockery and mugs are fine,' she said and Mia ticked them off. She knew all of this. The worst part was the kitchen. Her very expensive dough mixer was destroyed, as was one of her most precious things of all; her sourdough starter. Something which was not, she was devastated to learn, covered by the insurance. In fact, she prickled at the thought, the insurance representative appeared to smother a laugh when she'd asked. Even when she'd explained she'd had the starter for six years.

'Mia. Earth to Mia, come in, do you read me?' Ellie said, tapping her friend on the shoulder. 'I need your full attention. Yes. This situation sucks. And yes, it would be much easier if we didn't have to start from scratch, but we need to just get on with what we have.'

'Right.' Mia couldn't see how they were going to bounce back. For one thing the landlord had made it abundantly clear his allegiance wasn't to the café. He'd been approached by another local business to buy the building, at a reduced rate, but it would be off his hands. That meant Ellie and Mia couldn't be certain of the café's future – at least at the address they were at currently.

Ellie spoke over the dehumidifier that was on all hours to suck the moisture out of the air and put her hands on her hips. 'The fact is there's little else to do here for now. I'll take all this stuff,' she indicated the cups and other café paraphernalia around the damp serving area. 'I'll keep it in my garage, whilst we figure out our next steps. In the meantime we should carry on making the cakes we've got orders for. I'm sure you've got something you can be doing on that ball too?'

Mia nodded. She'd not replied to any of Will's texts since he'd come to the café two days ago. He'd said he'd give her a couple of days to think about what to do, but he'd repeatedly messaged to say she should talk to Ellie and she felt pressured. 'I'll take these to the car as I'll need them,' she replied, picking up the majority of her baking equipment.

Wrestling with the boot of Rose, her hand supporting the box of tools she used to put the finishing touches to her cakes, Mia considered her options. She needed to bake a wedding cake for the weekend, something which she was behind on. It was Thursday and by now she'd usually have the sponges prepped and ready to be iced. She'd have to work through the next couple of days to fulfil the order for the very sweet couple who'd requested it. They were getting married at the manor and Mia had been recommended to them many months ago. Fortunately they lived in London and had no idea of the disaster which had beset her these past couple of days. She didn't want them finding out either; she wanted them to have the perfect cake for their perfect day.

'Penny for them.' Liam had appeared at her side, and she blinked. She'd been miles away. 'Here, let me,' he said, taking the box from her so she could open the boot properly. He stowed the items precariously in the boot; which already housed a great many cups, saucers and her two cake mixers. 'I'll be honest, I didn't think you could get much in there, but that's quite impressive,' he said, grinning at her. Mia looked at Liam and frowned. He was being so nice to her, but relaxed when she saw his smile.

'You should have seen her when I moved into my flat,' Mia said, remembering. 'I had her packed with pillows, a duvet, so many boxes. There was a lamp sticking out of the rear window and I had to behave as though she was a wide vehicle whilst driving.' For the first time in the last couple of days Mia felt a smile work her way into her face.

'Her?' Liam said, his head on his side. He had, Mia realised, hair like the cherubs in Victorian paintings. His dark blonde curls fell erratically around his face, some longer than others, giving him a surfer vibe. He was wearing a thick military style woollen coat that came to his knees, a pair of jeans that looked like they'd seen better days and a pair of beaten up brown leather hiking boots. He had light blue eyes, and thick sweeping eyelashes that made him look almost feminine. Were it not for the strong square jawline.

'Mia, I said her? You've got a girl car?' he said, repeating himself and laughing. 'Does she have a name?'

Feeling hurt that someone would rib her just for being affectionate to her car, Mia slammed the boot down quickly. 'Yes, but only people who are kind to her get to know it.' She went to turn away from him but he put a hand out to stop her.

'Sorry Mia. I wasn't laughing at you. It was relief maybe? I don't know. My mum names her cars. I don't think I've met someone who does it other than her. I'd love to know this one's name,' he paused, looking deeply at Mia. 'If that's okay by her?' He let a small smile creep up on the side of his mouth. But it was a kind one.

'Rose,' Mia admitted.

'Ah, a rose by any other name would smell as sweet,' he said, grinning.

'That's...'

'Shakespeare, yes, and before you get the wrong idea it's because my sister was obsessed with that film. You know, with the angel wings. She had all these quotes in her room and around her mirror. You can't not take it in when you're confronted with it every day,' he said, grinning.

'I didn't know you had two sisters,' Mia replied, lamely, wondering why on one hand she would know, they'd barely exchanged more than two words in the last 18 months before the last week. Or why it mattered she didn't.

Liam shrugged. 'She's great. She lives in Spain and runs a bar now. Has a husband called Jose and a kid on the way. She's slightly older than me, but miles away as far as being a grown-up is concerned,' he grinned.

'She sounds like she's got it all sorted out,' Mia said.

'But she doesn't have a car called Rose, so really, who's the real winner here?' Liam replied, grinning again. His grin made something inside Mia flip-flop a little and she wondered what had got into her lately.

'Where are you taking it all?' he said, nodding in the direction of the boot. 'I can't believe I won't be seeing you guys in the mornings. It's been part of my morning routine.'

Mia smiled. 'We've enjoyed being part of everyone's routine. I can't imagine not being, and now...' she broke off. Liam didn't need to hear her woes.

But he raised an eyebrow. 'Now what? Come on, you can tell me.' He looked at Mia with such kindly concern, she relented.

'Now I need to bake a three tier cake – with three different flavoured sponges – and decorate it in less than two days, otherwise I'm going to have a very disappointed couple. But I don't have anywhere to bake it. I can't do it at home as it hasn't got a hygiene certificate.' She stuck her tongue at Liam's lopsided grin. 'Boring, I know. But I can't. So unless you know of a kitchen which has passed with flying colours, I'm going to have to confess to the couple that I won't be able to do their cake for them.'

Liam was silent and Mia admonished herself. Why did she think sharing her problems would be any better? He favoured Ellie to talk to, he didn't need her unloading her issues on him.

'You could work in ours? We have a space out the back of the shop. Mum is planning on opening a small deli soon, with home cooked sausage rolls and whatnot, so she's had a small kitchen installed. It's nothing like what you've had,' he rushed to explain as Mia smiled. 'But you should be able to get your work done in peace – and cleanliness,' he smiled.

'Are you sure? I won't be in your way, or your mum's?' Mia hadn't even considered what Liam's set-up was. All she knew was he worked at *Bananas*, and it was, now she recalled, a family business. She realised her own preconceptions were that "family" suggested he worked with his dad.

'Mum will be fine. She loves having people in the shop. The more the merrier. Though,' he reached to touch the sleeve of her coat gently. 'I would warn you not to act too interested in vegetables, she'll be sending you home with the odds and sods box if you're not careful.'

Mia looked at Liam for what felt the first time and felt warmed by his huge beaming smile. How had she missed him before? How had she overlooked such a kind, gentle, earnest human being?

Because she'd been preoccupied with herself, she realised sadly.

'Mia? Shall we? I can just carry this lot to the shop if it helps?' Liam was nodding towards her baking equipment in the boot. 'It won't take more than one trip to the car if we both do it.'

She nodded, watching Liam thoughtfully as he wrestled with Rose's boot.

Help came in the unlikeliest of places.□

Chapter Eleven

Two days of intense baking, cooling and decorating meant Mia had managed by the skin of her teeth, to get the wedding cake completed.

She'd worked two 18 hour days to put together all the decorations the couple had requested to cover the cake, which included hundreds of fondant roses made by hand, and many more tiny silver bells she'd moulded and sprayed. Her fingers ached from the miniature work and her eyes felt like she'd never be able to focus on something so delicate again. But the end result, even to her own critical eyes, was worth it.

Cascades of iced roses in a collection of creams and dusky pinks swept down the side of the cake, which had false tiers at the bottom to make it look taller than it was, and interspersed with this glorious meadow of roses were tiny delicate bells. She didn't know the reason for the bells, only that they looked pretty, but Charlie the bride had been insistent.

Mia stood back from the table she had been setting the cake up on at Shawford Manor and scrutinised it. She needed to add fresh roses, which would be delivered shortly, along with some eucalyptus, but until they arrived she'd done everything she could.

Mia almost jumped as Will came in. 'Sorry, didn't mean to startle you. They need to go there,' he pointed at the flowers which two young men placed down.

'We're just meant to deliver them, we're not meant to be doing any setting up.' The slightly older one of the two spoke causing Will to roll his eyes.

'Can't you just do it this time? We're a bit short-staffed in case you hadn't noticed.'

'Sorry mate,' the man said, looking the very opposite. 'Busy days Saturdays, we need to go and do more drop offs.' With that they both left, leaving Will eyeing up boxes which were releasing a very botanical scent into the room.

'Everything okay?' Mia asked tentatively, realising they'd not spoken since the flood. The cake had been her priority so she didn't know if he'd messaged her to think about Lee's offer.

Will turned and smiled, the shadows under his eyes telling the story. 'Sure, all fine.' Mia looked at the boxes of flowers and the undecorated room which said something different.

She looked up at him. 'Would it also be fine if I offered my assistance? I only need to add the flowers on here. Then I can help.'

Breathing a sigh of relief, Will pushed a hand through his increasingly volumised hair. 'I didn't want to ask, but honestly I've been so badly let down. This wedding was booked before I took over.'

'And before you got rid of most of the staff?' Mia reminded him. Will had the good enough grace to nod.

He held his hands up in defeat. 'Yes. But in my defence, I didn't know how much work was involved in putting on a wedding and I did try calling you loads of times but you didn't answer.'

'No-one answers the phone, why didn't you just message me?' Mia said, but she knew she wouldn't have answered those either. She had needed time, as well as being head down making hundreds of roses.

Will raked his hands through his hair again, looking sheepish. 'I thought you'd be mad at me, and I was right, wasn't I? Lee shouldn't have asked you to ditch your café to save my business, it was a mix up on their part and, I think we should just move on.' He smiled tightly. 'With that, frankly awful apology, can I say yes please to having help?'

Mia nodded. 'Yes, but we'll need more than us to get this place ready.' She looked at the undressed tables, the flowers, and knowing events always needed at least one extra hour to finish things off. The wedding reception would be held at the manor in just three hours. They didn't have any time to lose. 'Please tell me the catering staff are here?'

Will nodded. 'Yes, but the food isn't.'

'What?'

'I know. It's bad.'

Mia shook her head. 'It's worse than bad. Let's get this fixed.' She called Ellie, then, after thinking about it for a moment, Liam, to see if they could help. With both of them agreeing to come to the manor, and in Liam's case picking up the food which had been delivered to the wrong address, Mia set about organising the staff who were still employed at the house.

Two hours later and Mia beamed as she checked the main reception room. All the tables had been covered in crisp white tablecloths and the cutlery was shining to perfection. The delicate floral arrangements including white roses, white anemones and dusky green eucalyptus, were draped across the tables as per the instructions the original event planners had left.

'Where do these go?' Liam was carrying in enormous silver lanterns that were soon to be filled with church candles.

'Oh, outside. I'll help.' Mia came over and took one from him, grunting under the weight of it. 'These are not as light as you made them look.'

Liam laughed. 'It's all the potato sack carrying.' They set down the lanterns either side of the grand staircase at the entrance to the manor, just as Ellie arrived with six other smaller ones hanging from her fingertips. Liam continued to bring out an assortment of large and medium sized lanterns which Mia arranged so they were in groups.

'Something's missing,' she looked at the lanterns each with a solitary church candle inside. Even with those in the lanterns she felt it all looked a bit bare still. 'Ellie, do we have any flowers left?'

Ellie nodded and disappeared inside, reappearing a moment later with a box. She looked through the box carefully. 'There's a few odds and ends here, this was a wreath I think, which seems to have been damaged. But there are quite a few roses and strands of eucalyptus.'

Liam was looking around. 'Does this house have a vegetable or herb garden? I'm sure it would, you could add a load of rosemary in there too? It's dark green so will match the colour scheme, you can bend it so it'll fit inside the lanterns if you want, and it smells great when the guests arrive.'

Mia glanced up from where she'd been deconstructing the wreath and grinned. 'I love it Liam, if you can find anything to go in here and make it look just a bit more exciting you go for it.'

Ellie looked between the two of them, not speaking, waiting until Liam had walked off to the herb garden that Mia thought might be at the back of the garden.

'What's going on there then?' she indicated Mia and Liam.

Mia laughed. 'Absolutely nothing.'

Ellie raised her eyebrows. 'Right.'

'Seriously, nothing's going on.'

'Which is why the greengrocer is helping with your event? It makes sense you called me, but when did you get Liam's number?'

Mia realised she'd not mentioned to Ellie how helpful Liam had been the past few days, and that he'd given her his number should she need to get hold of him. If there'd been a problem getting into *Bananas* for example.

'He's just a good friend, that's all. And good friends help each other out when they're in need.'

Ellie pulled a face. 'A good friend who, as far as I'm concerned hasn't spoken to you for most of the last year and a half, okay.'

'Have I...do you...?' Mia hadn't wondered if Ellie was interested in Liam, she'd never given any indication that she was but then, she never showed interest in anyone.

'No, I'm not interested in him. In fact,' Ellie leant in to confide to Mia but just then Liam arrived with armfuls of rosemary.

'Here we go, this is exactly what we need. There was loads of it too,' he said, looking pleased with himself as he and Mia arranged the herb amongst the lantern display. Stepping back, and having turned on the battery powered candles, Mia smiled. Candles always made things magical.

'Thanks Liam, that's perfect.' All of a sudden Mia heard the crunch of tyres on the gravel drive and looked around to see a white London cab making its way towards the house. 'That must be the wedding party, we better disappear inside.' Mia made her way to the waiting staff, gave them a quick debrief of what was expected and headed to the kitchen, looking for Will. He'd said he'd ensure the canapes were made in time for the drinks, and she wanted to make sure he was on schedule.

Walking into the kitchen she grinned at the sight of Will, an apron tied around his waist and his sleeves rolled up, putting the finishing touches to a tray of canapes that a waiter took away quickly. He was supported by three other team members in the kitchen and she knew they'd be able to get the food out on time.

Looking up, his eyes met hers and he mouthed the words 'thank you' in her direction. Mia felt wobbly for a moment. There was something so touching about his whole demeanour.

He smiled, as though he knew what she was thinking and she hastily looked away.

'I better get back to it,' she said, walking quickly out of the kitchen, her heart beating hard. A huge grin on her face.

◻

Chapter Twelve

'To a terrific success,' Will held his glass of Champagne in the air ten hours later, as they watched the last members of the wedding party make their way out of the manor. The majority of the waiting staff had been sent home after 1am, leaving just Liam, Ellie, Will and Mia in the kitchen, finishing off dried up canapes and bottles of fizz.

'You were incredible,' Ellie said, squeezing Mia into a tight hug. 'I don't know how you managed it all.' Despite a blocked toilet, a bridesmaid getting stuck in a lift and the groom almost losing his speech, the reception had gone off relatively hitch free. The happy couple had paused on their way out so they could speak to Mia quickly. The groom, Cole, beaming with pride at his beautiful wife Charlie, as she hugged Mia closely and thanked her for the wonderful day that had been created. They were a little older than Mia had assumed they'd be. Closer to late 30s than early. But when Cole had referenced a second-chance at love, Mia realised they were marrying at just the right time.

Whether it was the Champagne on an empty stomach or the warmth at creating such a wonderful day for a lovely couple, Mia didn't mind. She felt happy and proud.

Ellie raised her glass and clinked it with Mia's. 'Cheers. Well done us.' She laughed, slumping down on a floral sofa which had seen better days. 'I'm famished,' she added, looking at Will who shook his head.

'We're out of canapes I'm afraid.' He looked around the kitchen but it was sparse.

Liam cleared his throat. 'Would it be odd if I said I had a dozen eggs in the van? We could have an omelette? There'll be enough scraps in the kitchen to turn it into something edible.'

Mia grinned. 'I think if it were anyone else, yes, it would be odd. But it's you, so it's not.' Liam smiled back and nodded.

'Right. I'll be back in a minute.'

The other three sat in contemplative silence, Ellie between Mia and Will. 'If your masked ball is half as good as today's wedding was, I reckon you'll have a success on your hands,' she said.

Will nodded, staring up at the ceiling. 'I hope so. The ticket sales are slow, I'm not sure it's going to work. I think we left it too late.'

Mia wasn't ready for his spurt of sadness after the elation of the day. 'You're so glass half empty. We've still got a fortnight, who knows where we'll be by then?'

'There's 200 tickets and we've sold maybe 120,' Will looked at her. 'If we can't sell another 50 at least in the next couple of days we'll have to pull the event.'

'I disagree. I think we'll be okay if we sell 120 in total. It's still enough to feel fun,' Mia argued.

Ellie looked between the two of them. 'Who's keeping an eye on the books for this?'

'He is,' Mia said, just as Will answered, 'she is.'

Both widened their eyes at each other. 'But you said you wanted to keep control?' Mia said, remembering their chat a month ago.

'No, you said you wanted to run the event totally. I took that to mean including the budget,' Will replied, anger making its way into his eyes.

Mia could feel tears starting to prick at her own. She was exhausted. Between the café's flood, the push to bake a wedding cake in a short timeframe, the wedding, and now the prospect that the ball wasn't going to happen. She wasn't sure she could face any more discussions with Will just then.

Ellie hesitated, then clasped her hands together. 'I'll do it. I'll look over the finances. I'll manage the budget and I'll have a look at where we might be able to shave off costs so that the masked ball can go ahead. It wouldn't look good for you to cancel it,' she consoled Will.

'But we can't ask you,' Mia broke off. Ellie's kindness was too much.

'Nonsense. You're not asking, I'm telling you. I may have tried to ignore our own finances lately, as I've been off the ball a bit, but I'm back. I know how stupid I've been hoping someone else will come and fix everything. I wouldn't let that happen to the ball.'

Mia furrowed her eyebrows, unsure, and Ellie continued. 'I know you took this job in a bid to bring in more cash to our business. But Mia it doesn't all need to be down to you. I'm your business partner. I want to be there with you every step of the way. It's not your responsibility to fix everything.' She clasped Mia's hands in hers and smiled.

'But the café...' Mia tried.

'May not be in our future,' Ellie said cautiously. 'It was my dream, and we tried. I love you for being there but maybe we need to see it for what it was, just a dream. Let's focus on our strengths and see where we are in a fortnight, after the ball.'

Mia still wasn't certain. Will seemed very quiet and all too quick to pull the event, which had been his idea in the first place. But with Ellie on board she did feel more confident. At least having her friend working alongside her would mean she wouldn't feel entirely alone.

'Deal,' she said, extending her hand to Ellie who grinned and grabbed it. 'Deal.'

'Will?'

He rubbed his face with his hands. 'I don't know. Part of me is worried this is all a terrible idea and I shouldn't have suggested it. The other part wouldn't mind seeing what we can do if we pull together, like today,' he admitted. Ruefully, he extended his hand to Ellie and shook it. 'Deal.

They all sipped their Champagne and Mia suddenly had a thought.

'Where's Liam?'

Ellie raised her eyebrows and looked at the clock on the wall. 'I don't know. He's been longer that I thought he would be.'

Will shrugged. 'Who cares? It's late and I'm not hungry anymore. He's probably gone home, which I recommend you two do as well.'

'It's weird he would disappear though,' Mia said, standing up and stretching, unsure why the other two weren't as concerned as she was.

'Not really, he's a grown man. He's got work in the morning, probably needs to be up early to get the best potatoes or whatever,' Will said. He was grinning but Mia wasn't keen on the tone he was using about her friend.

Ellie looked between the two of them. 'More likely he got to his van and decided he needed to go to bed, he's not the most sociable of people. He was probably feeling overwhelmed and tired.' She gathered her bag and coat. 'I think it's time for us to go too; I walked, so I'll need a lift,' she looked meaningfully at Mia who nodded.

'I just need to grab my bag from the other room,' Mia walked into the snug, the small lounge space off the kitchen that was once the servants' dining quarters. She collected her bag and returned to the kitchen, just in time to see Ellie and Will with their heads bowed in to each other, him holding her elbow as he leant in to say something. Mia coughed, unsure whether she was interrupting something, and they moved apart, Ellie blushing a little.

'About time, let's go,' Ellie said tying her belt around her coat and grinning, but the smile looked forced. Mia looked at them both and tried to work out what was going on, but Will wasn't meeting her eyes.

Mia nodded and followed Ellie, talking over her shoulder to Will. 'I'll come back tomorrow and we'll work out what we need to do with the ball to make it an absolute success.' Will nodded, looked like he was going to say something, then closed his mouth and just smiled.

Catching up with Ellie who was walking down the slightly shabby corridor that snaked its way behind the grand rooms, Mia tugged at her coat a little to slow Ellie down. ' What was that?'

Ellie shook her head. 'What? Me offering to oversee a budget? It's necessary. You and Will have got yourselves in a bit of a pickle. Nothing we won't be able to fix though, I'm sure.'

'No, I meant with Will. What was he saying?'

'Nothing.'

'It looked like more than nothing,' Mia prodded. They were still walking down the corridor and Ellie wasn't meeting her gaze. 'Tell me.'

Ellie sighed. 'I was persuading him he'd be right in carrying on with the ball, and putting his trust in us,' she smiled. Mia wasn't certain if her friend was telling the truth or not. She sounded like she was, but Mia had seen something. She was sure of it.

They walked out into the biting chill of the January night into the carpark and Mia shivered, quickly looking for her key whilst Ellie stood by Rose and stamped her feet to stay warm.

'How much have you drunk?' Ellie asked but Mia shook her head.

'A couple of sips of Champagne. Though I'm starving I could have done with the omelette.' She unlocked the door on her side, slid in and opened the passenger one from inside, Rose's lock often got stuck. Concentrating on de-icing the car, Mia turned the heaters up to full, all too aware the blast of heat did more to warm her face than clear the windscreen as it was stuck in the driver position. She really needed a new car.

'I wish there was a drive-thru round here,' Ellie groaned as her stomach rumbled and Mia laughed.

'Blame Liam. He disappeared. Eggs, of all things.' She laughed again.

Ellie was confused. 'Eggs? What do you mean?'

'Well, it's a bit of a random excuse isn't it? He could have just said he needed to leave.'

Shifting a little in her seat to get close to the heater, Ellie sighed. 'I told you, he probably changed his mind when he got to his van. It was too tempting to go home, and he'd had a full on day.'

Mia had spent a week with Liam and he'd never just walked away from something.

'What's wrong with him? You keep suggesting he can't handle things.' She fired up the engine and the car roared into life. Mia flicked the headlights on and drove slowly across the gravel drive.

'There's nothing wrong with him Mia; be kind,' Ellie chided.

'I am being kind. I'm just asking, what's his deal?'

There was a quiet in the car and then Ellie spoke.

'He's autistic. He's very low on the scale but he doesn't cope well with busy environments, or loud ones and he needs to control his surroundings,' she said.

Mia was shocked. 'He didn't say anything to me.' She tried to focus on the dark road in front of her, their town was bordered by woodland and countryside, beautiful but precarious in the middle of the night. It was a regular occurrence for deer to roam near to the town, so she kept her eyes trained on the road. The headlights offering small pools of light to help her.

Ellie blew on her hands. 'Why would he? And when would he? The last year you've barely paid him any attention. If you had, you'd have noticed he only came in when it was quiet, always ordered the same thing and kept his life small. It's what makes him feel safe. The fact he's been here today and done everything he has. It's impressive. You must have been very persuasive, his mum will be shocked.'

Mia had forgotten how well Ellie knew everyone. She'd been in the town for 15 years, and had met Ellie at secondary school there. But Ellie had grown up in the town and couldn't walk to the shops without saying greeting someone. Sometimes it was a gift, sometimes a curse. Mia couldn't be certain which she'd favour.

'I just don't know why he didn't tell me, I'd have been understanding,' Mia said quietly. She pulled into Ellie's road, found a place and parked up. Ellie wrestled with her seatbelt for a moment before it released her, then, after thanking Mia, opened the door allowing a blast of cold to come into the car. She almost shut the door, then changed her mind, reopening it and peering in to talk to Mia.

'I think he wanted you to get to know him without any preconceived notions you might have. Something I think he's achieved,' she winked and shut the door.

Mia sat in silence for a moment, thinking over the past few hours.

Shaking her head at what Ellie was suggesting, it was Will she liked, not Liam. Mia started the car and made her way down the darkened road.

Chapter Thirteen

The next morning Mia woke early and went to her kitchen. She found she could think at her clearest when she was up before the birds and her hands were kneading some dough. With the skill of someone who's been doing it for a few years, she pounded the dough, then left it to prove in the kitchen whilst she made herself a coffee and thought on the day before.

Her mind was swirling with thoughts of the masked ball. The odd way Will and Ellie were acting, and Liam's sudden disappearance. Mia's head was beginning to pound and she decided she needed a couple of painkillers to get it to go away. She knew she had some in her bag and picked it up from where she'd discarded it the night before. As she put her hand into the rucksack her hand brushed against something and she instantly knew what it was. Withdrawing it, she pulled out a pink note and smiled at the sentiment.

Being with you is my favourite thing

She stared at the piece of paper and shook her head. She'd left her bag in the room next to the kitchen all evening. Anyone could have had access to it.

But.

She looked up at her window thoughtfully, watching as dawn began to catch up with her. But Will was near it all evening. He hadn't left the kitchen – and if it wasn't him, then he probably saw who it was.

If it was Will, she needed to know why he was sending her notes rather than talking to her. And if it was him, what was the connection with Albert and his notes? They'd already ruled out this Albert being Will's grandad. But it was too much of a coincidence, as far as Mia was aware, that two men – with over 50 years' age gap – would both think of leaving her notes on pink paper. No, whoever was doing it was aware of Albert's notes, and either was copying him in a bid to be romantic or they were copying in a slightly more sinister way. A way which meant they were somehow trying to impersonate the old man. Mia shivered. It wouldn't be something like that. She was certain.

Noting the time, she returned to the dough, knocked it back, and shaped it into a small cottage loaf. She left it to prove again whilst she showered and changed and by the time she'd finished breakfast she'd been able to bake it and get it to cool. Wrapping it in a clean cloth, she decanted some fresh coffee into a flask, grabbed a pot of her homemade strawberry jam from the cupboard and, satisfied she had everything she needed, left the flat.

It was always deliciously quiet when she left her flat, but early on a Sunday morning it felt like even the birds had lie-ins. Shivering a little at the chilly January morning, Mia pulled her coat even tighter around her, enjoying the warmth of the jacket made for arctic temperatures but which her mum had declared would keep her from freezing on her early mornings into work. Mia smiled. She hadn't spoken to her mum for a couple of weeks and decided that later that day she'd get in touch. Life was so busy but, she acknowledged, that was no excuse to not give time to the woman who loved her more than anyone else in the world. In fact, she was Mia's biggest fan, had indulged her baking passion from the tender age of four, and always supported her business. If she hadn't moved to sunnier climes with her latest boyfriend, the two would still have been very close. Still, Mia thought, she couldn't fault her mum's reasoning. It was a lot nicer to live in Palma in January than the UK.

She arrived at *Bananas* and grinned. Unsurprisingly a light was on near the back of the shop. It had been the sort of constant she'd sought out whenever she'd walked to *Tiers of Joy*. In whatever the weather, however dark the morning, the light on at *Bananas* couldn't fail to lift her mood and make her feel like she had company. Even though her café was a couple of doors down, she had felt comforted knowing someone else was up and about.

Mia lightly tapped on the window and waited for Liam to come to the door. A chilly minute or so later and he came from the back of the shop, wiping his hands on a cloth which he stuffed into his pocket. He peered out of the window and looked surprised to see Mia.

'Morning, what are you doing up and about?' he said, with a level of worry in his voice. 'Not another problem with the café? I didn't notice anything.'

Shaking her head, Mia pushed the door a little further. 'Is it okay if I come in?'

Liam nodded. 'Sure, I'm just packing up,' he said, walking ahead of her towards the back of his store, Mia following in his wake.

'Tea?' he called over his shoulder and Mia grinned.

'Actually, I brought you something,' she said, pushing lightly past him so she could reach the kitchen counter. 'I baked this morning, I thought you might be hungry, and in need of a coffee after your very late night? With the café closed I thought you could do with it.' She pulled the loaf out of her bag, placed it on a board and retrieved the jam and butter too. She added the flask. 'We just need a couple of mugs and plates.'

'Mia, this looks amazing,' Liam looked surprised. 'But why did you?' Realisation dawned on him. 'Oh, Ellie's said something hasn't she?'

Mia considered lying but decided it wouldn't be right, she nodded. 'A little.'

Liam shook his head. 'I wish she hadn't. Now you're going to treat me differently,' he said with sadness.

'I won't.'

'You will, you already are, baking for me, bringing me a coffee because sad little Liam can't cope without his routine. Is that what you think?' Anger sparked in his eyes and Mia was surprised.

'I was just trying to be kind,' she replied, 'it was a way of saying thank you for all your help yesterday. It meant a lot to me you were able to help. I thought I'd repay the gesture, but if it's unwanted.' She began to pack the jam in her bag and Liam laid a hand on hers, causing a zing of excitement to zip through Mia's entire body and confusion to etch itself across her brain.

'Ignore me. It looks good. It's a kind thing to do,' he said, still gruff, but smiling. Noticing his hand was still on hers, he took it away quickly. 'But I don't want it every day, I'm not having you feel sorry for me.'

Mia laughed. 'As if. I'm not getting up at 4am to bake you bread every day,' she said, slathering butter on the slices of granary bread, followed by dollops of strawberry jam containing soft but entire fruits.

Liam cleared a bench of boxes of fruits and vegetables he was putting together before delivering them across the district later that day, and indicated she should sit down. Mia handed him a mug of coffee and a plate containing two slices of bread and jam.

There was a silence as they both ate and drank companionably. Mia, sated, warmed her hands on her mug.

'I'm normal you know,' Liam said, as he wiped his mouth with hands. 'You don't have to treat me differently.'

Mia smiled. 'I know, as I said, this was just to say thank you. But also,' she stopped, hesitating over the thing she wanted to ask.

'I knew it. You were literally buttering me up,' Liam grinned, before stuffing the rest of the bread into his mouth. 'What do you want?'

'Can I carry on working here for a bit? Just until we know what's going on with the café? I've got cakes to bake and I'm still finishing up things with the masked ball.' She looked at him with hope.

He frowned, crushing her spirits. 'Why don't you ask Will? He's got a decent enough set-up over at the manor house with that big kitchen. There's not much room here.'

'I know.' Mia found she couldn't frame her reasons for not wanting to spend all her time at the manor house, but she knew she needed some space from Will. 'Hey, Mia,' Liam said, as he placed his mug down carefully on the kitchen counter. 'You've dialled out.' She looked at him, his head on one side as though trying to figure her out.

She realised she'd gone red. 'Sorry, just...thinking,' she finished lamely.

'About the lord of the manor?' Liam said, then clasped his hands together and batted his eyelids at her. 'Oh Will, you're so handsome, I just want to kiss you,' he said in a high voice.

'Is that meant to be an impersonation of me? I don't sound like that.'

Liam pushed her gently. 'Don't huff, just jesting a little.' He shifted a little, as though uncomfortable. 'You like him though, don't you?' He stood a little too close to her, and Mia wondered what to say.

'Sort of. Maybe,' she replied quietly.

Liam nodded. 'I thought as much, it'll be his posh boy accent that's got you going.' He grinned. 'Oh Mia, I *must* ravish you in the parlour.' He spoke in the worst attempt at an upper class accent Mia had heard.

She swatted him lightly on the shoulder. 'That's enough of that,' she said, as they stood, barely centimetres apart. She was suddenly aware of the heat coming through his t-shirt where her hand still lay on his bicep, the texture of his thick cotton t-shirt grounding her, reminding her where she was. Mia heard Liam's breathing in sync with hers and she caught herself. What was going on? Quickly she removed her hand and stepped back, swallowing hard.

'I think you might be right. I...maybe...I should work at the manor,' she said quickly, trying to cover her flustering.

Liam looked hurt. 'What, really? Why? You can definitely work here Mia, I was only joking,' he said. 'You can fancy whoever you like,' he added. Mia wondered if she saw pain flit across his eyes, but pushed it away. She was imagining things.

'No, I've changed my mind. I...' she began packing up her bag, throwing the flask and bread remnants into it without care. 'I've got to go.' Mia got up and walked away, tying her coat's belt tightly at her waist.

Just before she left, she turned to see Liam hadn't moved from where they'd been standing and his face was twisted with shock.

Mia bit her lip. She was walking away.

Chapter Fourteen

'Two days until the big day then love,' Sam said as she bustled into the room where Mia was simultaneously trying to glue diamantes and feathers onto masks, whilst attempting to have a measured conversation with the unhelpful customer service person from the company that was meant to be supplying the lighting for the event.

'But they were due to arrive yesterday; they can't arrive in three days' time. The event will be over with by then,' she said, exasperated as the person on the other end offered up excuses about logistics and shipping. 'No, I want to speak to your manager's manager. I need this fixed now,' she said, almost shouting into her phone.

'I'll come back,' Sam said, moving as though to beat a hasty retreat to the door through which she'd just arrived.

'No, wait,' Mia shouted to her, but with a smile on her face. 'I need you, stay.' She looked back at her phone. 'Not you, you're not going anywhere; get me the manager please. No, don't put me on...' She looked forlornly at the phone. 'Hold...honestly I'm not sure if today can get much worse.'

'Come here love. Hug?' Sam opened her arms and Mia stood up for the first time in what had to be hours and hobbled over to her. Falling into her and smelling the familiar scent of Chanel and chocolate, she squeezed her friend back.

'Okay, that's made things feel a bit better,' she acknowledged. 'Why are you here? Other than to give out hugs of course.'

Sam walked Mia to a chair and plonked her down. They were in what used to be a study, but over time when it was under the council's tenancy it had been turned into a very nondescript office. Pine desks and cheap black office chairs still littered the room, which Mia had taken over as her headquarters. Everywhere Sam looked there were items needed for the event.

A rack of black and red costumes hung on a rail, waiting for the staff to wear. There were bags of feathers in shades of red and pink that were, presumably, about to be stuck onto or into something and, Sam squinted to see if she was right. 'Is that crate full of chocolate truffles?'

Mia nodded, a small smile creeping across her face. 'Yes, but you haven't seen them, okay?' Even though she'd put a pin in discussions around the chocolate café, Lee had still sent over a specially created chocolate for the masked ball. At this point, Mia was happy to have any support. Though the chocolates wouldn't last long with Sam around.

Sam raised an eyebrow, trying not to salivate at the contents. 'You have my word.'

'Right, now, why are you here? Come to lend a hand?' Mia asked hopefully and looked crestfallen when Sam shook her head.

'Not yet. I will, I want to help, but I want to tell you something,' she started, then paused.

Mia frowned, it wasn't like Sam to consider her words and if she didn't start talking soon she'd have to hurry her up. Mia's to-do list was six pages long, and that was just for today. 'What's up?'

Sam breathed in, as though to get confidence, 'Tony and I are getting married and I wanted you and Ellie to be amongst the first to know,' she squealed, an enormous smile on her face. 'It's because of your café that we met. I know its quick, before you say anything, but we're both getting on and we don't want to waste a moment of our lives. We've found each other, how lucky is that? And we don't want to lose one another,' she laughed as Mia pulled her in for a celebratory hug.

Mia shook her head and smiled fondly. 'I'm so happy for you both.' It was a shock, the speed which they'd got together. Hadn't they been flirting for just a few months? She wasn't even certain they had been on any dates. But then, she didn't keep tabs on Sam. And she was old enough to know best. 'I'm really pleased.'

Sam beamed. 'Like I said, when you find the one, all you want to do is hang on to them.'

Mia nodded. 'How did you know?'

'What?'

'How did you know he was "the one" for you?' Since the incident with Liam she'd steered clear of the greengrocer shop, in a bid to get her emotions in check. She wasn't certain what had passed between them, but she was sure he wanted more than just friendship. Whereas Mia was sure she had feelings for Will. A person who had been noticeable in his absence the past couple of weeks. She'd begun to wonder if he'd given up on their event, she'd seen so little of him. In fact, she was only just holding it all together. She was certain if someone asked her how she was she might cry.

'Mia, is everything okay?' Sam said, realising her young boss had gone very quiet and pale.

'I think it's all going wrong,' she replied, blinking to try and keep the tears away. Sam looked around.

'With this? No, you've got it, it's going to be amazing, it's the talk of the town,' she said with joy but this gave Mia only further horror.

'See, people are expecting something incredible. I don't know if I can even deliver so-so right now,' her breathing was erratic. 'Will seems to have all but disappeared. I see him briefly most days but it's like he's steering clear of me. And Liam...' she broke off, not wanting to think of his look of hurt as she'd walked away.

'That was the other thing I wanted to talk to you about,' Sam said gently. 'I don't know what's gone on between you two, but Tony was saying he was talking to Liam's mum and he's not happy. He's turning up at work late, he's being rude to customers. The other day he swore at an elderly lady for wanting strawberries.'

'Well, it is February,' Mia said with a grin. 'Hardly the season for them.'

Sam shook her head and patted Mia's fondly. 'What are you like? What I'm saying is, when you two were friends Liam was the happiest Cynthia has known him in years. But now you've fallen out, she's worried about him.'

Mia bit her lip. 'I see.'

'Do you?' Sam pressed.

'Yes, I note that everyone is concerned about Liam, but not about me. As far as I'm concerned, he's a grown man. How he deals with emotions is nothing to do with me. If you don't mind, I've got a lot on. Is that everything?' She stood up, indicating the conversation was over, purposely ignoring the look of shock on Sam's face.

Rolling her shoulders back, Sam stood carefully, as though considering her next move both physically and verbally. 'Don't push everyone away Mia. Loneliness is the worst place for someone to be.'

'Goodbye Sam.'

Mia turned away and walked back to the pile of feathers, listening to Sam's footsteps disappearing as she headed out of the doorway. Looking down at her phone she realised it had, at some point, turned off, effectively cutting the call she'd been trying to have with the lighting supplier.

Back to square one. Again.

Slumping into the feathers, Mia put her head in her hands and cried.

'Ahem.' Snuffling, Mia looked up, and saw Sam looking down on her. She wiped her nose with the back of her hand.

'This is a big job, you need to have help. You don't need to do everything on your own you know,' Sam said, then knelt down beside her, wincing. 'You have no idea how painful it is with these knees. 'Tell me what you need doing.' She sat beside Mia.

'I have help, I have Ellie,' Mia reminded her, behaving like a sullen teenager.

'And that's great, but that's just two of you, why not let the rest of us get involved too?'

'Rest of...?' Mia said, but as she spoke, Tony came around the corner of the room.

'I didn't hear anything,' he said with a cheerful grin. 'But what you need to know is Sam has told me I should lend a hand. And what my Sam wants, she gets,' he said, looking at his fiancée with such warmth, Mia couldn't help but feel compassion for them both.

'Any good at sticking feathers?' she asked, holding up the glue gun.

Chapter Fifteen

'All I'm saying is she needs to know,' Mia heard Ellie talking to someone as she walked into the kitchen at the manor. She needed to finish the cake she'd made for the ball, and, knowing that decorating was her happy place, her way of calming down, she'd brought herself to the kitchen in the hope she'd begin to feel better.

Casting a furtive glance in Ellie's direction, she saw her friend quickly putting her phone in her bag. Instinctively realising she shouldn't have overheard the end of the conversation, Mia concentrated on tying her apron around her waist and pulling the plastic box which held all her cake decorating tools towards her. The three tier cake stood iced but unfinished. She did what she always did when she was at that point of a cake design, she lightly stroked the icing, noting the cool, hard, shininess that the covering had. It had hardened overnight, as she needed it to, giving the cake underneath a good level of protection. Her next move was to add the many feathers she'd piped the day before, and left to dry. She'd also made a mask out of black fondant, decorated with edible diamonds. The effect would be, she hoped, flamboyant, sexy and fun; everything she wanted the event to be.

'Right boss, what's next?' Ellie arrived by her side. 'I've got the boys from one of the moving companies coming in to help us shift the furniture, to ensure we've got enough room for dancing.'

Mia unpacked the last of her supplies. 'Great. The stage is being delivered today, so I could do with you keeping an eye on that, making sure nothing goes wrong there but it's not due for a couple of hours. The decorations need to go up, but Sam and Tony are working on those, and I need at least three hours of uninterrupted time to finish this off,' Mia said pointedly. 'Oh, and someone needs to place all those toppers on the cupcakes. Any idea who could help with that?' .

Ellie rolled her eyes. 'I better have a very good time at this ball,' she said meaningfully.

'Have you got an outfit sorted out?' Mia said as she began to prepare the icing she would be piping onto the cake in luxuriant swirls before placing the many delicate iced feathers.

Wiping her hands on a towel, Ellie nodded. 'I do – though it was slim pickings in town. I think everyone that's coming has had the same idea.' She unsealed the boxes of masks Mia had made the day before that were going to adorn the cupcakes. 'These are cute. Anyway, I went to the charity shop – you know the one with the wedding dresses?' She spoke, not expecting Mia to reply, so used to the methodical and quiet way her friend chose to work. 'I went in there and found the most gorgeous burgundy wedding dress, so I'm wearing that.'

Deciding she needed to stick to the colour theme of pink and red as well, but aware she couldn't be expected to move around in a massive dress, Mia had opted to wear a well fitted black suit, accompanied by a bright pink tie and matching high heels. She knew already the heels would be a nightmare on the day and she'd end up with raw feet, but the overall look was something sexy, fun and, she hoped, screamed events planner, so she was willing to risk blisters.

'Have you got a plus one?' Mia asked, absentmindedly, aware that unlike herself who would be there in a professional capacity overseeing the whole event, Ellie would be attending as a guest. Able to enjoy a few glasses of Champagne and some of the delicious hors d'oeuvres Mia had agreed on with the catering company. And she could bring someone with her to enjoy it with.

'I might have,' Ellie said, fishing out some more of the cupcakes to add to the pile she'd decorated already. 'But they haven't confirmed yet.'

Mia frowned and looked at her friend. 'You're being remarkably coy about this – who are you going with? And would I approve?'

Ellie grinned. 'Actually, you do know them. I hope you'll approve.' Looking as though she was about to say who she was going with, Mia waited to hear, but they were interrupted by Will coming in carrying three boxes of vegetables.

'I can't see where I'm going,' he said, his voice muffled as he made his way into the kitchen. 'Where do I put these?'

'Not here,' Mia shrieked as he got very close to her cake. 'Ellie help him,' she ordered as she threw herself between the boxes and the cake.

Ellie quickly jumped into action and retrieved one of the boxes from Will, so he could see, and placed it on the side away from the cakes. Mia watched as he placed the other boxes down alongside Ellie's one.

'Cheers Ellie,' he said, patting her arm a little awkwardly, then bending himself backwards a little way to stretch out his muscles. 'I said to Liam I could help out, so he gave them all to me. I could carry them, but negotiating my way through the passages was a nightmare.'

'Liam was here?' Mia said, and Will turned to look at her, as though noticing her for the first time.

'Yes, but not for long, I think he was busy.' He looked around the kitchen reminding himself of all the tasks ahead. 'How are things looking?'

'Did he seem okay?' Mia tried to concentrate on the cake, not wanting to give anything away. Sensing Will's eyes on her, she looked up.

'Who? Liam? Fine, why?'

'No reason.'

'They've had a falling out,' Ellie said, as she carried on decorating cupcakes. 'I don't think they're talking to each other.' Mia flashed her a look. 'What? I know you Mia, you didn't think I would find out? I'm just surprised you didn't tell me.'

Will, watching the interaction between them just shook his head. 'Okay, I'm not going to pretend I understand what's going on, but if you could run me through what's needing doing, I'm here.'

'Finally,' Mia uttered under breath, forgetting she would be heard.

Furrowing his brow, Will looked at her warily. 'What was that?'

'Nothing. Ignore me.'

'No, if you have something to say, you may as well say it,' Will said, his hands on his hips.

Mia matched his body language and faced him. 'Okay. Where have you been these last few days? I've had to manage all of this by myself. No offence Ellie,' she said to her friend who was about to say something. 'But I needed you here. Everyone else is pitching in now, but I needed you; it's *your* event,' she added, frustrated.

'Which I'm paying *you* to pull together,' Will pointed out. 'If you don't think you can hack it, without pulling in all your mates, maybe I need to look for someone else to work with,' he raised his eyebrows.

Mia's heart raced. She was so angry. 'I think it's worth reminding you that I only said yes because you needed helping out. I felt sorry for you,' she lied. 'I don't need this.'

'Fine, so you don't want a full time events planner role? No of course not, you've clearly got loads of options.' Will practically spat his words out. 'If you must know, I've been in discussions about the café I'm bringing here.' There was a sound as Ellie clattered a knife to the floor.

'Sorry, butter fingers,' she said, looking between the two of them. 'I really don't think now is the time for you to fall out,' she suggested, returning to decorating the cupcakes.

'No Ellie,' Will said loudly. 'It is the time. There's a lot going on right now, and I think Mia and I need to discuss it all.' A silence stretched between Ellie, Mia and Will, until he shook his head, giving up. 'Fine. I'm going to help get the stage built, tomorrow we'll talk. I'll be here tonight as the press are coming and I want to make a good impression. Don't mess this up for me Mia.' He left the kitchen.

Watching Will walk away, hot tears leaked out and Mia quickly wiped her eyes. She looked to the ceiling to compose herself. 'I can't believe he's going ahead with a café here, another competitor.' She shook her head. 'Ellie? Did you hear me? I said another competitor.' Her friend's head was bowed over the cupcakes as she meticulously applied the tiny masks to each one, accompanied by edible jewels and feathers.

Ellie's voice came quietly. 'We don't even have a café Mia. We don't have the money to look for new premises. It might not even be an issue. We might have to face facts we may not have a café together again.' She shook her head then continued with the decorating. 'I can't believe you've just done yourself out of a job. You couldn't have just remained civil to him?'

Of all the people in the world, Mia could have sworn she could count on Ellie, but even she was disappointed in her.

Chapter Sixteen

Later that evening, all thoughts of disappointing Will and Ellie disappeared as Mia walked into the ballroom and pinched herself. It was as though a fairy-tale had come alive. Women in gloriously decadent dresses, ruched silks, layers of velvet and strings of pearls adorned with matching masks in varying degrees of subtlety, swept past her, dancing with their beaus. Mia grinned as she recognised the owners of *Cuts Above* dancing past in hers and hers matching dresses. Their masks were the same design but with the colours reversed. They were laughing and, Mia realised with relief, enjoying themselves.

In fact, everywhere she looked people were laughing, drinking, dancing, chatting, and generally having a good time.

The hours of sticking feathers and designing the event had paid off too, with the effect being one of a decadent, Moulin Rouge-esque room, full of baroque touches. It was not subtle. It was a big, bolshy, rich affair in varying tones of burgundy, pinks and gold and it screamed Valentine's, without looking as though they'd fallen into a Disney film. Everyone had worn a mask too, Mia noted, as she rearranged her pink lace one which matched her tie and shoes.

All the men were in black tie, but they'd found masks to fit the occasion. Black leather ones, half face Phantom of the Opera style ones and even a few very ornate Venetian ones adorned faces. It was funny, despite a few people who'd made themselves known to her, Mia didn't know who most of the guests were due to the anonymity of the masks. Though, that had been the point. Privacy afforded. A chance to let loose and enjoy oneself for the evening. Not that she was expecting anyone to make a spectacle of themselves, she smiled, they hadn't prevented people bringing their phones in – she had numerous places set up for Instagram worthy moments that she hoped people would capture on camera.

'Hey, this looks amazing,' Lee, the chocolatier came over in an incredible draping cream mini dress, showing off their killer thighs, accompanied by a pair of the highest heels in bright pink that Mia had ever seen.

'More like *you* look amazing, what an outfit. I've no idea how you walk in those though,' she said nodding in the direction of their stilettoes.

Lee laughed. 'Lots of practice. I just wanted to say, I'm so sorry with the whole café thing. Will called me the next day and I was just so embarrassed.'

Mia frowned. 'He called you?'

'Yes. Will did. After your visit? Told me all about the mix up. But like I said, it's all my fault. I hope you can forgive me? Will said not to call you, he was going to explain? Though I get the impression maybe he's not?'

'Erm.' Mia was going to reply when her attention was taken by a commotion by the flower wall, a sumptuous creation from one of the local florists, who'd weaved in flowers of every type in pinks and reds, entwined with twinkling white fairy lights. 'Sorry Lee, I have to go. Have a good evening,' she called over her shoulder as she realised there appeared to be some sort of altercation between a woman in an organza red dress and what appeared to be a scruffy looking man without a mask.

Rushing over to find out what had happened, Mia instantly recognised the poorly dressed man as Alex the journalist from the *Mistlebrook Gazette*. Plastering on as big a smile as possible, Mia wedged herself between the two who appeared to be ready to start a brawl.

'What's going on?' she said through gritted teeth. 'Do we need to do it here?'

'He snuck in and was taking photos of us all, he's a...pervert,' the woman in the red dress said angrily. 'Some of us want to just enjoy this place in peace.'

Mia recognised the woman as Linda, the quiet head librarian who she'd rarely heard say anything above a whisper. Then turned her attention to Alex who was looking sheepish. 'Is that true? Have you been taking photos?'

The man nodded. 'But I didn't sneak in, I was told I could come for free by Will. When I did the interview with you,' he replied quickly.

'Why don't you go and help yourself to a glass of bubbly,' she suggested to Linda. 'I'll handle this,' she mollified, throwing a sharp glance at the reporter. Waiting for Linda to walk off, she smiled again, this time a little more warmly.

'There's no issue with you being here Alex, in fact I'm thrilled you're here, as long as it's to cover the event in a positive light,' she forced a laugh. 'But you can only take photos of people who give you their consent. I want to encourage an air of abandonment here, a place for people to leave their cares at the door and have an evening of pure joy.'

Alex grinned. 'Can I quote you on that?'

Mia smiled back. 'Yes of course. And maybe you could let me check the photos before they go to print? Just to be on the safe side?' She hoped he'd say yes, she knew he wasn't obliged.

'Of course,' he grinned. 'On one condition.'

Hoping it wasn't anything too difficult, Mia nodded. 'Go ahead.'

'I don't suppose you have a mask do you? I feel decidedly underdressed.'

Mia smiled. 'I just so happen to have a spare on me,' she laughed, always prepared. She handed him a black and white mask she'd deliberately ordered in case someone was without.

'Thanks,' he said, the relief in his voice. 'If it weren't for the brown suit I'd look like everyone else.' He nodded in the direction of the room, and Mia realised what he meant. Everywhere she looked all the men looked alike. All black suits, white shirts and black bow ties. The majority had similar masks too, mainly black, rarely ornate like the women's. Here and there a slightly different one with a striking pattern on it stood out. But for the most part, every man looked the same. Not the women though. The women stood out for their exquisite dresses. It was a scene Mia thought she'd never forget.

She hadn't seen Will for hours, though she'd been receiving texts from him letting her know that food was on time and leaving the kitchen. Mia had to admit she'd been impressed by his timekeeping, as plates of canapes circulated exactly on schedule. They'd barely spoken since their argument earlier. She felt she needed to offer an olive branch so unlocked her phone and tapped out a message.

Come out of the kitchen and see this. I think all the hard work has paid off.

Mia pressed send and looked around. She'd not heard from Liam for a few days now, and was sad he was missing out on the event. He'd been so helpful with it all, she felt he should have come too. But his mum said he wasn't up to it when she'd spoken to him earlier that day and she didn't want to press it. Pausing to consider whether it was a good idea or not, Mia composed a short message and sent one to him as well.

You should come to the ball. The music is great and you might even like the food. Some of it has tomatoes in it.

So cringe. She hoped he'd find it funny. The idea that a greengrocer would come out for an event to try vegetables. Still, she'd sent it already. There was no use amending it.

Her phone dinged.

I know. I've had ten.

Mia frowned, Liam was here? She looked around and couldn't spot him. But if he was dressed like the majority of the other men she wouldn't be able to recognise him, she realised. Knowing she needed to do a turn around the room to check everything was running as it should, and ignoring the fact it might help her spot Liam as she did so, she began walking.

A few stray feathers had fallen to the floor, so she scooped them up, concerned they'd stick to a shoe and cause someone to slip. Her hands full, Mia decided to leave the ballroom briefly and pop them in a bin. She stepped out of the room into the corridor, the sound of the revellers dimming as she did so, and walked straight into the solidity of a man in black tie wearing a black leather mask that covered the top half of his face and went back over his head, concealing his hair.

'Sorry, didn't see you there; bit dark,' she apologised. Then realised she was still pressed into the man's chest, could feel the warmth through his shirt. He smelt familiar and Mia smiled but before she knew what was happening, the man had leant down and was kissing her gently on the lips.

Fireworks exploded in her head as they kissed deeper and Mia felt her head tingling with enjoyment.

Suddenly there was an enormous bang that wasn't in her head, and the lights went out.

Chapter Seventeen

Shrieks came from the ballroom and Mia, leaving her anonymous kisser in the corridor, dashed to the room, turning on the torch on her phone.

'What's going on?' one woman yelled in her face, whilst another grabbed her. 'I can't cope in the dark, I freak out,' she hollered.

Mia looked around, with no clue as to what had happened but, feeling the sense of apprehension and claustrophobia which comes with a power cut, knew she needed to take control. She quickly tapped out a message and pressed send.

Power cut. Can you check fuse box?

She sent it to Will and hoped he was okay in the kitchen.

Unless it had been him in the corridor of course.

Shaking her head to rid herself of the kiss she'd just had with the masked stranger, she decided to make her way to the stage area, with no real idea of what to do. As she reached the stage, the crowd began to quieten and she could feel the eyes of 200 people on her. Spotting she had a torch on, many of the others held their phones up as well, each one shining a light into the air. By the time Mia had reached the stage, a prick of a tear came to her eyes as she took in the sight of 200 lights waving in the dark. It was beautiful.

'Hello everyone,' she said, as loudly as she could. 'I wanted to thank you all for coming to our event, which will hopefully be the first of very many to come.' There was a smattering of applause. Looking out at the lights, she was struck with an idea. 'I know this moment of darkness might have come as a surprise to you all, but it's our way of creating something magical. Special. Unusual even. Think about it, how often have you stood in the dark with 200 others?'

There was a swell of laughter as the crowd warmed to her, and calmed down.

'We rush around so much. We do so much in our days, we often forget to soak in the moment. To take stock of what, and who, we have around us. Now's your chance. Take a moment to remember this evening and if you want to introduce yourself to the neighbour next to you.'

She heard murmurings as strangers introduced themselves and laughter began to trickle around the room.

Mia checked her phone and breathed a sense of relief as she read the reply from Will.

Should be up and running again soon

'Now, ladies and gentlemen. How about a song? Something to raise this roof and bring our voices together? She was stumped for the moment. What song? What would people know? Then it came to her. A song lyric written on a pink note by an old man looking for company. Tentatively, and knowing she sang like a banshee, Mia breathed in.

'There's nothing you can do that can't be done,' she began, and breathed in a sigh of thanks as others recognised the Beatles song, joining in with the rest of the verse. Just as they hit the first line of the chorus 'All you need is love', the lights came back on, lighting the space and showing Mia a room full of smiling, happy faces. Instead of stopping when the lights came up, everyone continued, encouraged by the band who struck up an accompaniment. When it finished they all cheered, bringing a bubble of laughter out of Mia she hadn't anticipated.

Allowing the band to carry on with their set list, she slipped away from the stage, hoping to find her anonymous kisser, but everywhere she went people stopped her to tell her what an inspired moment the "dark bit" was. Worrying when she spotted the journalist coming towards her and assuming he'd worked it out as a calamity which had been narrowly missed, she braced herself for his interrogation.

'Inspired. That's definitely going on the front page,' he grinned, patting her on the back then disappeared into the throng. Mia shook her head, thrilled at the way things had turned out.

'What a laugh,' Ellie caught Mia by the hand and whirled her around. 'You kept that quiet didn't you? You could at least have let your friend know, I screamed so loudly.'

'I thought I recognised someone,' Mia said, giggling with relief as Ellie spun her again, 'and anyway, it wasn't planned. Will had to fix the fuse,' she laughed at the look of horror that crossed her friend's face.

'Was he okay?'

'Who?'

'Will? I'm assuming he hasn't gone up in a puff of smoke?'

Mia shook her head. 'You're a worrier. He messaged me just before to say he was sorting it. Anyway, I'm on way there to check in on him,' Mia said, deciding now wasn't the time to let Ellie know about her anonymous kisser, or the conclusion she'd come to that it could have been Will.

'Well, you had me fooled, that's for sure,' Ellie said, spinning Mia around once more.

Laughing, Mia reluctantly came to a stop. 'I need to check a few things,' she said, excusing herself.

'Have fun,' Ellie blew a kiss before walking off. 'Don't work too hard.' Mia watched with longing as her friend disappeared into the group of people enjoying the evening, wishing she was part of it, but proud that she'd been able to create something that gave so much joy to others.

'Tell me, was it you who made these cakes?' A shrill voice that could cut glass was talking to Mia from within an ornate white pearlescent mask, but it was one she'd recognise anywhere. Will's mother, Alicia.

'Yes Alicia, I did.' Mia waited for the inevitable tongue lashing she was about to get, her arms folded. Ready to leave as soon as the older woman was through.

'Well my girl, they are quite simply the most exquisite little morsels. Utterly delicious, tell me, could you rustle up say 300 for a women's luncheon I'm organising at the end of the month?' Alicia asked, smiling.

Wrong-footed, Mia stood looking at Alicia with her mouth wide open.

'Close your mouth dear, we do not need you catching flies,' the woman said, raising her eyebrows above her mask.

'Erm, sure. I mean, yes. I can do those cakes for you, just give me a ring. Will has my number,' Mia stammered out quickly, grinning. 'Thanks.'

'Off you go then.'

Mia realised she'd been given her orders and did as she was told, moving as quickly as was polite out of the ballroom once again and began to walk down the corridor. There was no sign of her mystery kisser and she wondered for a moment if she'd imagined it. She pressed her fingers to her lips. No. It had happened. The pressure of his lips on hers, the pleasure, the scent of him. Walking into the kitchen, and narrowly avoiding a waiter with yet another tray of Champagne, she looked for Will.

'Will, are you around?' she called.

One of the chefs who was wiping down the sides now the evening was drawing to a close, pointed to the snug next to the kitchen space. Mia smiled, nodded her thanks and smoothed her hair down with her hands. A little nervously, worried she wouldn't know what to say to him now he'd made his feelings clear, she walked around the corner.

It didn't take long for her brain to catch up with what her eyes could see. But still Mia made no sound. There, locked in a tight embrace, an un-masked Will was kissing Ellie, and by the looks of it, they weren't planning on coming up for air any time soon. Noting the discarded black leather mask on the beaten up sofa, Mia shook her head in disgust, then backed away.

She didn't know what to say. Or how to say it. What she did need to do was to get out of the room, and as quietly as possible. Without them knowing she'd seen them.

Walking quickly back through the kitchen, the chef who'd pointed Will to her, raised his eyebrows at her swift departure.

'Find him?' he asked, as Mia knocked into the side of one of the large ovens, catching herself on the hip, she was in such a rush to leave. She hastily nodded; and left as quickly as she could.

Walking as fast as possible back towards the ballroom to convince herself that Ellie was in fact in there, and not kissing the man she fancied. Mia noted many of the revellers were on their way out the front door. The clock had struck midnight, the official end of the evening.

Accepting the praise and thanks lavished upon her as she bade farewell to many tipsy, unmasked party goers, Mia nodded and smiled as best she could.

She'd cry when she got home.

Chapter Eighteen

'That's the sixth time you've looked at your phone in five minutes.'

Mia looked at Liam, who was attempting to mimic her bread making technique and was punching down some dough. It was Sunday. Two days since the masked ball, and he'd arrived unannounced with two decent coffees and a request to learn how to make bread, so he could bake a loaf for his mum as a surprise.

'She gets sad over Valentine's, Dad left the same weekend about five years ago,' Liam had confided.

'Not too much, it still needs to resemble dough,' Mia cautioned, putting her hand on his to stop him as he pummelled his dough a little too hard.

'So, what's going on? Why the constant phone checking?'

Mia shaped Liam's dough and carefully placed it on a tray, covering it with a light plastic bag she kept aside for her home baked breads, so it could prove for another hour or so. Neither had mentioned their fallout from the week before.

'Ellie keeps calling. I keep ignoring,' Mia admitted, sitting back down on the sofa she'd made into her camp since the ball had finished and pulling her well-loved once red blanket over her legs. Liam plonked himself next to her, stretching his long legs out in front of him and crossing them at the ankles.

'Okay, and why are we ignoring? I thought she was your best friend?' He looked at Mia, his eyes a little too intensely focused on her.

Mia rolled her eyes. '*We* aren't ignoring her. I am,' she replied, a little petulantly. 'And really it's nothing to do with you Liam.'

Taking a deep breath, he put his arms behind his head, fully relaxed. Mia noted his biceps flexing as he did so, the sleeves of his white t-shirt peeling upwards to show them off.

'Isn't it?'

Mia looked at him. His blue eyes, and his casual smile. He looked at peace. Something she craved.

'It's nothing to do with you. I just...' she broke off, remembering seeing Ellie and Will. 'Thought something had happened with someone, and when I realised it might have happened with someone else I was confused...and I realised after maybe I didn't want it anyway...but now...I don't know.'

He looked at her, a sad smile tugging at his mouth. 'What happened exactly?'

Mia shook her head. It was silly. Stupid even. The whole anonymous kissing incident. If it was Will, he'd been playing her and Ellie along the whole time. But that didn't seem like him. Did it? But if it wasn't him, it could have been someone else. She looked at Liam. He was smiling at her, his head on one side, his profile suddenly very familiar.

'It was you.'

'What?' He bit his lip briefly, a sign he was uncomfortable, but Mia had to know, and she knew what she needed as evidence.

'Let me smell you.'

Liam grinned, sitting up a little. 'Smell me? What, like a perfume sample? No thanks,' he laughed and moved away to the end of the sofa.

'No, come here, I want to smell you,' Mia said, softening her tone and smiling. She knew she'd recognise her kisser if she got close enough to him. She knew she'd recognised it at the time.

The familiarity. She moved closer to Liam, who didn't move this time. Just stayed stock still. His chest lifting with every breath. Moving into his space, ever so slowly, Mia leant in towards his neck and inhaled. The scent made sparks dance across her head again at the familiarity. Liam still hadn't moved, and Mia leant closer, inhaling the scent of his hair, the wax, the shampoo he used, her stomach filling with butterflies as she did so.

'Liam,' she whispered, and as he turned to look at her, finally, achingly, for the first time in the last five minutes, his lips brushed hers and instantly it felt like she was home. As though they'd kissed like this a thousand times over, not the once. Mia sat back, shocked at the familiarity.

'Why?'

Liam shook his head. 'I don't know, it was something to do with the anonymity of the mask?' He looked bashful. 'Honestly I thought you knew; I assumed you'd guessed who I was. That was why you kissed me.'

Mia opened her eyes wide. 'I didn't kiss you; you kissed me, and no, I didn't know who you were...' she scrabbled for the words, some sort of explanation why kissing a stranger was okay. Then realised she didn't need to justify it.

'You knew it was me?'

Liam nodded. 'Of course. You were the only one bossing everyone around with a walkie-talkie attached firmly to their hip,' he grinned. 'You knew it was me. Of course you did.'

'No. I,' she faltered.

'Wait. Did you think...?' Liam moved away from Mia, standing up quickly to gain more distance. 'You thought it was someone else. You *wanted* it to be someone else, to be Will.' Realisation dawned. Liam shook his head and moved away, throwing his jacket on and picking up his phone as Mia watched, frozen to the spot. 'You thought you were kissed by the lord of the manor, when in actual fact you got the lowly greengrocer. Poor you.'

'Liam. No. Wait, that's not it,' she stuttered, watching as he made his way to the door of her flat. But he was right. She had thought it was Will. Until she saw him kissing Ellie. Even then she hadn't confronted Will to find out whether he'd kissed them both on the same night, preferring to shove her head in the sand. Now Liam, this wonderful, kind, caring man, was leaving her. After the most intense kiss she'd ever experienced.

Liam stood at the door, visibly angry, his body shaking.

'I thought you knew. I thought I'd shown you in enough ways how much you meant to me – even if I wasn't able to say it to your face. I trusted you Mia,' he turned away and opened the door. 'You don't need to worry, you won't be hearing from me again.'

He left, slamming the door behind him, leaving Mia to collapse in a ball of tears and recrimination.

How had everything gone so wrong?

Chapter Nineteen

'Ellie,' Mia tapped on her friend's door with hope, rather than expectation, that it would be answered. After ignoring Ellie's calls and texts over the weekend and spending all of Sunday in a flood of tears, she'd come to the realisation that she may have lost the potential of one relationship, when Liam walked out, but she wasn't losing the other most important one in her life. 'Ellie, I'm really sorry,' she spoke through the door, 'Ellie, I'm not going to go until you open the door.' She listened for any noise behind the door but cursed its thickness. 'I can't leave cakes just out here. Who knows who'll eat them?' She paused, then stooped down to the letter box, carefully holding the box of cakes as she did so. 'I made salted caramel chocolate brownies. I know they're your favourite.' She listened to the door.

'What are you doing?'

Mia almost fell over, startled at her friend appearing behind her. She seemed to be in gym wear, not something Mia had seen her in before.

'I,' Mia stood up, and proffered the white cardboard box to her confused friend, 'I've made you a batch of apology brownies,' she admitted, 'because I'm a terrible friend and you deserve better.' Ellie gave her an odd look, but reached past her to put the key in the lock.

'You best come in and explain.' Ellie led the way, throwing her key into the faded bowl she'd brought back from South America a few years ago, its pattern once bright, now faded. Ellie walked into her tiny kitchen, turned on the overhead lights and filled up the kettle, before placing it on her gas stove. Mia watched as she lit the flames with a match and smiled.

'One day you're going to have to join the rest of the world and use an electric kettle,' she grinned.

Ellie looked nonplussed. 'No thank you, I love the smell of it this way. Makes me think of my grandma.' She pulled out mugs Mia recognised from their many years of drinking tea together, throwing in teabags as she did so. Mia watched as Ellie filled up a small watering can and gave her houseplants on the crammed kitchen window a drink, before following her into the lounge where large cheese plants, succulents and peace lilies adorned small tables, nestled amongst piles of books. Everywhere she looked, there were mementoes from Ellie's travels, and her love for all things bright. Patchwork cushions in a myriad of colours, clashed with woven blankets in bright teals and limes. Table lamps dotted the lounge, hidden behind plants, or sat on piles of books. It should have felt claustrophobic, but Mia only ever felt it was homely and welcoming.

'I'll bring the tea in,' Ellie said, disappearing back into the kitchen after watering the rest of the plants. Mia could hear the kettle whistling and grinned, she always did like the sound of it, much as she ribbed Ellie for being old fashioned. 'Here we are,' Ellie said, as she re-joined Mia, and placed the tray of tea on a low dark oak coffee table, along with plates for the brownies she was now looking expectantly at Mia for.

'Oh right, here you go,' Mia dutifully opened the box and laid the six delicious brownies on the plates, watching as Ellie's mouth turned up. She never could say no to one of them.

'So, where were you this morning?' Mia asked as Ellie bit down on the thick slab of brownie, and her friend laughed.

'Great timing,' she said through a mouthful, before washing it down with a swig of tea, 'I was at tree yoga – where were you?'

It was Mia's turn to look surprised. 'Why were you there? You hate yoga – you hate exercise,' she reminded her friend who laughed.

'I was there to find you. You've been so weird all weekend, I didn't know what was going on. I thought if I went to that woo-woo yoga in the woods you love so much, I'd find you there and discover what's going on.' She looked at Mia keenly, 'what *is* going on? From what I understood, you had a very successful event. I saw you on Friday night and it was all fine, and then suddenly you don't take my calls, my texts are unanswered? I thought maybe you'd hooked up with someone, and you didn't want interrupting, but we usually let each other know we're safe at least. I was worried,' Ellie said.

'I,' Mia began, but Ellie held a finger up to shush her.

'I went round on Sunday,' she grinned, 'but saw a certain gorgeous grocer walking into your block of flats with coffees, and I thought "oh, now I see what's been going on". I'm thrilled for you – for you both, but I am hurt you didn't let me know you were okay, and you didn't let me know that you and Liam got together.' She took a bite of the brownie, 'these are too good Mia. Don't let me eat any more,' she said, taking another and placing it on her plate, 'after this one.'

'I missed yoga,' Mia replied, 'I was so caught up with everything I actually missed it. That has to be the first time in months,' she realised.

'Six,' Ellie confirmed, 'the teacher was quite concerned, said you were her most diligent pupil. Frankly I found it all very cold and wet.'

Mia grinned, but was annoyed with herself. She knew part of her self-care routine had to include her time surrounded by nature. Committing to her yoga in the woods once a week gave her a central point to focus on. She vowed to return the following week, whatever was going on in her world.

'So, what's going on with Liam?' Ellie looked at Mia with a small grin on her face and Mia felt her insides churn with embarrassment with how she'd handled everything. She shook her head.

'No. I need to be honest with you first,' she took a deep breath in, then told Ellie all about how she'd kissed someone at the ball, that she'd thought it was Will, that she'd seen Ellie and Will together and how, as of yesterday, she'd realised it was Liam she'd kissed. And how she'd managed to ruin all chances of being with him. 'So I avoided talking to you because I wasn't certain how I felt about you and Will. And I was sad you'd not told me you were together. And confused because I thought I was falling for Will.' She looked down at the ground. 'You let me think I had a chance with him.'

Ellie looked as though she was struggling with what to say, then let out an exasperated sigh.

'The whole world doesn't revolve around Mia Jones,' Mia looked up at the sharp tone, 'it doesn't. Which doesn't mean I don't love you completely, and doesn't mean I wasn't terribly sad for you when Jake left. I was. I saw you through those dark days, didn't I?' Mia nodded. 'And I kept our business going, just. Even when it was apparent your eye was off the ball. But a few months ago I was delivering cakes to the manor house, you couldn't do it because Rose had broken down and I bumped into Will. We just got chatting and hit it off,' Ellie's eyes sparkled as she remembered the meeting. 'You were still sad, and not up for doing much outside of the café, yoga and being home. But I was craving a bit more of a life. Will asked me out for dinner. I said yes, and well, for the last few months we've been seeing each other,' Ellie exhaled.

'But why didn't you tell me?'

'Because you were so anti-men and we'd made that pact, hadn't we? I didn't want you to feel like I was ditching you in favour of one, and honestly?' Ellie looked at her keenly, 'the longer it went on, the harder telling you became.'

Mia's face burned with shame. She'd been so caught up in her own world, she'd not been aware her friend was in a relationship? How self-centred was she?

'But Will? The masked ball? What was that all about?'

Ellie breathed in again, as though for strength. 'I could see where things were heading with the café, not the flood I must add,' she said hastily, 'but the sales weren't good and our profit margin was getting smaller. I was talking to Will and he happened to mention he was thinking of events at the manor. I knew you had a background in them, so I put you forward. I thought at least that way if we did have to close the café, you could do a job you love and still bake cakes for the events. He wasn't sure, to be honest, but the more he's got to know you, the more impressed he's been.' Ellie smiled to reassure Mia, 'but his kindness to you was only ever that. In fact, he was keen to tell you about us for weeks. The stress has made him sharp with you, hence your argument the other night. He was concerned you were getting the wrong idea with his interest and we'd decided to tell you after the ball when things weren't so stressful. Though of course, you went awol for a bit.'

Mia's mouth opened and closed. It was a lot to take in.

'Did he tell you about the job offer? The café?' she asked. Again, Ellie nodded.

'It would seem Lee got the wrong end of the stick, Lee thought you were me when Will arrived with you. I've since been in discussions with them and have accepted the role as manager of their café at the manor,' she admitted, casting her eyes downwards.

Something solid landed in Mia's stomach. And it wasn't the brownie. 'So that's it then? No café? It was your dream.'

Ellie smiled grimly. 'It's a tough business. I'd rather have less stress, and let someone else worry about their investment. I love running a café, meeting people, baking. But I don't want the stress of whether there's any money left at the end of the month. I just need a wage. Lee can offer me that, and I get to put my own stamp on the place.' She cocked her head on one side. 'Are you upset with me?'

There were a lot of things Mia was feeling. Hurt, betrayal, jealousy. But she knew in her heart of hearts that Ellie was being realistic. Running the café had been good but it had been a lot of stress and not a lot of reward. The only thing that made it worthwhile had been talking to her lovely customers.

She shook her head slowly. 'Not upset. Just...overwhelmed a bit,' she managed. 'Iit's a lot to take in.'

Ellie nodded. 'And you? What are you going to do? Will was thrilled with the masked ball and he says he's already getting lots of requests for other functions to take place there. He's keen for you to become full-time event manager at the manor, if you'll accept; he says he's very sorry for the argument. Everyone wants a bit of the Mia magic.'

Mia's head was throbbing with everything she was being told. 'I think I'll need some time to consider it,' she managed. 'Full time? How will I fit in the cakes?'

'Which cakes?' Ellie asked, confused.

'The ones for the events, and the café,' Mia said, unsure.

'Originally we had thought you'd be able to combine the two, but with so much interest it seems you'll be very busy with just the events. You could pick and choose which big cakes you did if you really wanted to, but the day-to-day ones in the café I'd have to look at getting someone else in. You can't do all of it, you'll never have a chance to sleep,' Ellie laughed.

'Right,' Mia said. She knew it was good offer, a concrete job. One which would provide security and she didn't want to be ungrateful. But she'd have to give up the majority of her baking. 'I'll need a bit of time to think things over,' she reiterated and Ellie smiled.

'Of course. Will and I were hoping you would join us for dinner at the manor this Friday. Nothing fancy, we're thinking delivery pizza. You could let Will know your decision then? You could even bring Liam, bit of a double date,' she grinned.

'I don't think Liam will ever talk to me again,' Mia admitted.

Ellie looked surprised. 'Well, he didn't talk to you for 18 months and that didn't stop him from liking you. I'm sure you can figure out a way to make amends,' she looked at Mia in the way only a friend who really knows you can, 'if that's what you want of course.'

Mia smiled. She didn't know what she wanted anymore. Her whole world felt like it had slipped on its axis.

Chapter Twenty

'Come on girl,' Mia panted, wiping the sweat off her brow. She was wrapped in a thick bright blue scarf, the fluff pushing into her nose, and the windscreen was fogging up with her breathing. But she needed the engine on for the heating to work, to stop the fogging, and right now, she couldn't get the engine to start. So she was an odd mix of cold, sweaty and frustrated. 'Just go will you. Start.' She turned the key in the ignition and crossed everything for the car's engine to kick into action. But nothing.

Resting her head on the steering wheel, Mia tried to work out what she was going to do. She needed to get to the Red Hat Society to deliver her box of cupcakes she'd promised them. They'd been contacting her telling Mia how much they missed meeting at her café and chatting with the regulars, but especially her super creamy cupcakes. So she'd offered to pop by to one of their homes, where they were holding their meetings for now, to drop in a few. They'd been delighted and told her they'd pay, of course. So she'd made a big effort. Whipping the buttercream with lilac food colouring so each cake was adorned with a thickly piped swirl of icing, and adorned with a tiny red hat of fondant that she'd made the night before. She'd been pleased with the end result. The little hats stood proudly on each of the tuffs of icing, causing the cakes to look like an army of slightly squat, very well dressed ladies. She knew the red hatted ladies would be amused by them.

If she could get there.

'Come on Rose. Just start, there's a good girl.' The engine kicked in and Mia quickly put the car into first, sending thanks up to the car gods, relieved when she got to the end of her road and was able to keep going. She was convinced the next time she came to a stop it would be the end for her car.

There was an odd "phutting" noise coming from the exhaust, but Mia pressed on, driving as carefully and controlled as possible. However, with just a few streets to go before she reached the address she'd been given, she had to stop at some traffic lights. Almost as soon as she put the car into neutral she heard a tell-tell sign of the engine cutting out. And if that wasn't bad enough, a cloud of very black smoke began to appear from under the bonnet. 'Oh Rose. What have you done?'

Suddenly, Mia realised she shouldn't be in the vehicle, and after hastily grabbing her cakes and bag, leapt out of the door. Other cars had begun to file round her, honking as they did so.

'It's on *fire*, what do you want from me?' Mia yelled as one particular man held his hand down on the horn the whole time he was going around her. Getting to the pavement as quickly as possible, Mia looked around to see if anyone could help but she realised the only sensible thing was to call the fire service. Whilst she talked to the operator and reassured them that she was standing far away from the car, though many other drivers seemed oblivious to it, she watched as thick black smoke belched from under Rose's bonnet and hoped it didn't explode.

Standing on the side-lines as she watched the fire vehicle arrive and a team of heavily fire proofed individuals jumping down, she felt mortified by the attention. Especially when they cordoned off the area and doused her poor little car in so much foam it resembled more of a boat than a Mini.

'You're lucky you weren't in there for much longer,' one of the fire fighters came over to speak to her. 'Are you okay? I'm Laura,' she said.

'I'm fine. Just shocked,' Mia replied honestly and Laura smiled.

'That's normal. Your car clearly fancied a little drama in its life.' She looked at the group of people watching them. 'Is there anyone you can call? I'm assuming you need a lift somewhere? Home?' She looked down at Mia's hands and Mia followed her gaze to where she was still gripping tightly onto the box of cupcakes.

'Erm, no, I was meant to be giving these to…' She stopped, there was no way she'd get to the red hatted ladies. She'd have to call them and apologise. But she knew they'd understand. 'Would you and your team like a cake? To say thanks,' she said, giving a small smile as Laura beamed.

'Lads, the lady here wants to give you all cakes. None of you are on a diet; are you?' She smiled as the men filed over and each took a cake, thanking Mia as they did.

'Looks like an extreme way to get promotion,' Alex from the *Mistlebrook Gazette* had appeared out of nowhere but he was smiling in a kind way.

Mia looked over in relief. 'I'm just glad they stopped the fire getting out of hand.'

'End of the road for your car though. Excuse the pun,' Alex said, grinning. 'Any going spare? I haven't had lunch yet, got told to cover a "major vehicle fire". Not that it seems it was all that major.' Mia handed him a cake and watched as her car was loaded on a tow truck.

'Feels major to me,' she sniffed, trying not to cry. 'I loved Rose. Now what do I have left?' She spoke quietly, as Alex looked at her with concern, clearly unused to dealing with women crying.

'You have these, and they're amazing,' he said, 'indicating the cakes. I was telling my editor about those cinnamon rolls you gave me the first time we met. And the cakes I had at the ball, I was pitching you as the next food editor; I reckon you'd be brilliant. It's not just for our paper, it would be for the whole group, and a magazine. I mean, it's not *The Times*, but it's a start,' he grinned. 'What do you think?' He took another cake.

Mia stared blankly at him. 'I don't know, I'm...uh...I might be giving it up to run events,' she said, feeling odd with the words that were leaving her mouth.

'What?' Alex had his mouth wide open, un-chewed bits of cake dropping from his lips. 'No, you can't. That's mad. You're a genius cake maker and if you don't do it.' He shook his head. 'Surely it's your calling?'

Looking at him, Mia pondered what he was saying. 'But I can have security if I take the job,' she replied and watched his face for a reaction.

Wiping his mouth with hands, and shoving them in his pockets, Alex looked at her earnestly. 'I didn't get into local journalism for the money. I did it because I enjoy meeting people, writing about them and finding out what's going on. I hope to one day become a national journalist, maybe even work for the BBC. But I don't make much money. Sometimes it's not the be all and end all. Surely if you have a skill like yours and you love doing it, you should continue? What's the phrase? A day doing a job you love is a day not working? Or something like that. Don't give up your dream Mia, it's the only thing that separates us from the animals,' he smiled. 'Do it because you love it, not because you have to.'

He brought his phone out from his pocket. 'I better get a picture of this sad scene, so that the editor believes me when I tell him it was not a mass vehicle fire. I'll still file it as something though. Maybe *car fire leads to bake sale* as a headline?' he said, laughing as he pointed out a few people who were hovering near to Mia, holding cash.

Mia grinned and bade farewell to him. Shaking her head at the money being offered, she doled out the cakes and walked away back towards her flat.

Alex was right. She couldn't take the events job. But she didn't know what the next step would be.

No car. No café. No support from Ellie. No Liam.
She needed a plan.

Chapter Twenty-One

'So are you looking for another Mini?' The salesman who had looked with concern when she'd arrived walking up the lane usually reserved for tractors and farm machinery, stood in front of Mia in the draughty barn that housed 15 or so used cars. He looked pointedly at her wellies caked in mud and raised an eyebrow. 'Nothing to trade-in?'

Mia smiled tightly. 'I'd love another one, but I imagine my finances won't stretch that far,' she admitted. The insurance company she'd spoken to after Rose was taken away as a burnt out husk had agreed a small pay-out, but it wasn't going to get her a new one. She looked around. The day was dark and wet and none of the cars looked all that appealing. Spiderwebs clung to the dark grey Ford Fiesta closest to her and she wondered when the last time was that someone had actually bought a vehicle from *Cars!!!* Mia made a mental note not to buy from anyone in the future who added an exclamation mark to their business name. Let alone three.

'So?' The salesman stuck his hands in his pockets and raised his eyebrows at her. 'What shall we look at?' He was roughly her age, but his slightly worn suit and shabby appearance served to age him by at least ten years. He'd introduced himself as Ted and had followed her around from the salesroom to the warehouse, as though expecting her to steal one of the cars there and then.

'A run about I suppose?' Mia said, uncertain now she was here. She'd never bought a car alone. She'd bought Rose with her mum years ago and hadn't made any of the decisions or been involved with the bargaining to get the price down. The whole process felt alien to her and Mia wished she'd brought Ellie along. But she'd made the three mile journey out of town on foot and she wasn't coming back empty handed. 'Lead the way,' she said, with more enthusiasm than she felt.

A little while later it was apparent she wasn't going to find something at *Cars!!!* Whilst there'd been a couple of contenders, they were either too old and unlikely to run for much longer, had too many miles on them, or were out of her price range.

Dejected, she accepted the under brewed tea from Ted back in the salesroom, and let out a sigh. 'Don't worry, we get cars in every week. I'll take your number and give you a call. I know what your budget is and what you're looking for,' he said kindly. 'I'll try to give you the best price I can.' He grinned.

'What?' Mia felt self-conscious.

Ted shook his head. 'Nothing.' He cleared his throat. 'Oh go on then, you're her aren't you? The one who had the café in town? Ran that incredible ball?'

It was Mia's turn to raise her eyebrows. 'Yes, well I used to run the café. It's closed now. How do you know who I am?'

Ted laughed. 'I suppose that did sound a bit weird. My mum is a member of the Red Hat Society. She used to go on and on about you and your cakes,' he grinned. 'She was devastated when the café had to close. Says she has nowhere to go now with her friends.' He looked sad. 'She was so depressed when Dad died. It's okay, it was a few years ago,' he interjected before Mia gave her platitudes. 'Those ladies picked her up and made her happy again, but they didn't have somewhere to go together for coffee, your café was perfect.'

'Oh, I see,' Mia was downcast. So now she was responsible for a widow's happiness?

'I think she liked how kind you and the staff were more than anything else. She liked that when she arrived on her own you'd know her and talk to her. Staved off the loneliness a bit,' he smiled sadly. 'She won't come and live with me, but I do worry about her being lonely,' he admitted.

'What's her name?'

Ted shifted. 'You're going to laugh.'

'Try me.'

'It's Hattie,' he grinned. 'Hattie from the Red Hat Society. Couldn't make it up, could you?'

Mia clasped her hand to her mouth. 'Hattie's *your* mum? Oh she's lovely, so kind. I loved seeing her and hearing how she was.' Suddenly Mia remembered something. 'Oh you're the one getting married,' she said, smiling as the puzzle pieces came together.

Ted nodded. 'She mentioned me?'

Mia grinned. 'She's so proud of you. Told us all about her wonderful daughter-in-law, and that her Ted had made a very good choice.' Mia remembered Hattie's celebration that her son was getting married. She'd insisted on buying cake for everyone. 'Hang on, aren't I meant to be making you a wedding cake?' she asked, then put her hand over her mouth again. 'Ignore that. I think it was meant to be surprise.' Ted laughed.

'Knowing mum she's insisted on some sort of wild theme? She doesn't know why we want to keep the wedding neutral. According to her it's boring. She claims we need colour in our lives.' He leant a little closer to Mia. 'Can you do me a favour? Make any cake you like, but maybe keep it to one or two colours? We're more a white icing, simple decorations kind of couple.' Mia remembered then what his mum had asked for. A completely white cake with simple decorations. And inside vivid blue, yellow and pink coloured sponges. She wasn't convinced Hattie would move from the brief.

'So when do you reopen?' Ted asked as he poured a little more tea out of the pot into her mug.

Shaking her head, Mia accepted the mug once again. 'Not, I'm afraid. It's too expensive and the landlord is selling up. The new owner doesn't want us. It's all over, my business partner has chosen to work elsewhere.'

Ted smiled. 'It's a shame you won't reopen, but hey, maybe it's time for a different direction?'

Mia nodded. 'Maybe.'

'Actually,' Ted hesitated. 'Look, I've got an idea. It's not here yet, I bought it in an auction and it's due to be delivered next week, but it might be the answer to your work and car worries,' he said tentatively, looking at Mia to gauge her opinion. She didn't say anything, so he pulled out an iPad from under a pile of papers and tapped the screen a few times to find what he was looking for. 'Here.'

Ted turned the screen around and Mia smiled at what she saw on screen.

'Oh,' she breathed. 'She is beautiful.'

Smiling and nodding, Ted tapped on the screen so Mia could see more pictures of the VW campervan in a zingy bright yellow. Instantly, it felt as though she'd found her soulmate and every part of Mia longed for it.

'What if you converted it, and you turned it into a sort of café on wheels?' Ted suggested, as he showed her the interior. 'You could add a marquee for the hotter months, and on the colder ones you could park outside of venues that don't have cafes, so that people like my mum and her group could still enjoy your coffee and cakes but at different places across the county.'

'Like a fast food van? On the side of a road?' Mia was incredulous, the idea of frying bacon for white van men didn't appeal all that much. She was shocked when Ted roared with laughter.

'No, I was thinking something a little more...you. Something like this,' he said, tapping the screen and typing in the search bar. Ted showed her a few images of VW vans that had sides which opened up, showing people working inside, serving drinks and coffees. Some had tall chairs propped up against the hatch, giving somewhere for people to sit and chat. On one the whole roof raised up, with a blackboard attached to show the menu of the day.

Mia grinned. 'I love it. My own café, but on wheels.'

'I bet you could do some covered events in winter too, like those antique fairs. Or that place with the wood fired pizza,' Ted mentioned, reminding them both of the large barn space in the town a few miles away which invited local food vans to park up for a day or a week. People would come to them, all undercover.

Excited, but realising she had to be realistic, Mia sat back. 'It's going to come at a cost though.'

Ted nodded. 'Of course.' He looked at his screen. 'It's looking like it'll be £15,000, and then you're looking at probably £10,000 to deck it out.' Mia winced.

'I don't think that's going to be possible.' She stroked the picture, then shook herself. 'Still, it was a nice idea.' Realising she'd finished her tea, she stood up. 'I should probably be going.'

'I can give you a lift if you like? This weather is dreadful, just give me a minute to get my stuff together.'

Mia nodded and took herself out to the covered porch to watch the rain pour down. She couldn't get the idea of the VW out of her head although she knew what Eliie would say. It was a crazy idea. But, she countered, it could serve as her kitchen space too, somewhere to bake and design her celebration cakes. She didn't have enough room in the flat and she needed a solution soon or she'd be penniless.

But she couldn't afford it.

Mia exhaled and tried to ignore the tears threatening. No, she'd buy a sensible small car and then she'd find some premises to bake in.

Then why was her hand taking her phone out of her jacket pocket? Why was it tapping out the details of what Ted had shown her? Looking up conversion costs?

By the time Ted had closed up, Mia had made a decision. She was buying Tulip; that was the name she'd given the campervan already. She'd apply to the bank for a business loan.

Watching the dull green of the countryside zipping past in a blur as she was driven home Mia daydreamed about what having Tulip could mean, then, overcome with worry, realised she hadn't said anything to Ted. 'Don't sell her...the campervan I mean, don't sell it. Not yet. I'd like to look into buying it. Just give me a few days to see if I can secure a loan. And, um, I hope you don't mind me asking but, erm, is it your best price?' She hated having to negotiate but remembered her mum's car buying advice.

Fortunately she realised Ted was smiling from ear to ear and didn't look the least bit put out from her asking. 'I've been thinking about it. If you can promise that the Red Hat Ladies will get a visit from you once a week, I'd be willing to sell it to you for the auction price.'

'Really? And how much is that?' Mia kept everything crossed.

Ted rolled his eyes. 'Don't let anyone know I did this or it'll be bad for business. I paid £8,500 for it. How does that sound?'

Mia shrieked and hugged Ted, causing him to beep the horn and laugh at the same time. 'I could kiss you. Really?'

He nodded. 'Really. I think it's worth it. You could say it was an investment in my mum's happiness. But no kissing, my fiancée wouldn't be pleased. Neither would that chap by my guess,' he had pulled up outside Mia's flat and had nodded in the direction of a hunched figure trying to stay dry under the small porch, his jacket pulled in tightly around him. Who was now looking at Mia getting out from a car, where moments before she'd been hugging another man.

She ran over to Liam as he shoved his hands in his pockets, looking as though he was thinking about leaving. 'Don't go. It's not what it looks like,' Mia said breathlessly, waving Ted away and miming she'd call him. 'He's my business guardian angel. But before I tell you about my big plans, why are you here?'

He looked at her. 'I forgot something last week. I came back for it.' His voice was clipped. Sullen.

Her heart plummeting, Mia had been convinced he'd come to make up, she nodded. 'Okay, what was it?' She didn't remember him leaving anything in her flat, but moved a little nearer to him to unlock the door and let him in.

They were in such close proximity she had brushed her hand against his, and could feel his warmth. She looked up, raising her eyes to meet his.

'This.'

Leaning in, Liam gently pushed a lock of her hair away from where it was sat on her cheek, his thumb lightly grazing her skin as he did so, sending sparks of electricity across her skin in its wake. She stayed stock still as his hand rested at the nape of her neck causing her body to tingle with his touch. Mia realised she was holding her breath, waiting for what she hoped was about to happen. Her eyes locked on his.

He bent down a little and kissed her achingly gently on the lips, before pressing into her and kissing her deeply, all the while his other hand entwined in hers.

Chapter Twenty-Two

'You didn't forget anything then?' Mia said, smiling as she lay in her bed with Liam, tracing patterns lazily on his chest with her index finger. He turned his head and smiled, before something passed across his eyes.

'What?' Mia hoped it wasn't bad news, she'd decided things could only get better and nothing was going to change that.

Liam pushed himself up onto his side so that his head was propped up on his hand and he could look at Mia.

'There's something I need to tell you,' he said, carefully choosing his words. Mia went to speak but he held his hand up. 'If you don't mind, I'd rather you just don't say anything, until I've said what I need to say. Okay?' Nodding, Mia mimed zipping her mouth shut and smiled in encouragement, hoping her heart hammering in her chest wasn't audible to him. She had no idea what he was going to say but she was hoping it wasn't something like he was moving away. She had a sneaking suspicion she had fallen hard for Liam.

He exhaled. 'Okay, right.' He sat up, shrugged his shoulders a little and exhaled, causing Mia to feel more than a bit nervous. 'So, the thing is. Albert was my grandad. Mia's mouth opened wide in shock.

'Albert? As in my regular?'

Liam held his finger to his lips. 'Shush, you said you'd wait to hear everything first,' he told her and she nodded. 'So, Alberts...was,' he corrected, 'was my grandad on my Mum's side. He lived in the care home by the park. He would come to your café, have a drink, come to see us and then go home. He was very old, 94, when he died. But his wishes were that he just slipped away. He didn't want an announcement in the paper or a big funeral. He said it was wasted money to spend it on him when he wouldn't enjoy it. So when he died, that was that.'

Mia frowned and Liam nodded. 'I know. You're wondering why I didn't set you and Ellie right about who he was. But the thing is, that was his wish too. He said he enjoyed being "just Albert" when he was at your café, enjoyed the anonymity and the buzz of people around him. Said it made him feel alive to hear the chatter and to enjoy your company,' he smiled at Mia. 'But the thing is, Grandad was a bit of a meddler. Or tried to be. One day, about a year ago, he said he'd seen your ex kissing someone in the park. He didn't recognise the woman, no one from the café, but he knew Jake was wrong for you.' Liam looked at her as Mia pulled the duvet a little closer to herself, trying to figure out what this all meant. 'He asked me to let Jake know that we knew he was cheating on you. I told him he needed to tell you and do the right thing.' Liam shook his head as he remembered. 'Next thing I knew he'd upped and left you.'

Liam took a sip of water. 'Grandad was really worried about you, we all were you know, all your regulars,' he smiled. 'You don't know how vital you and Ellie were to us all. Your warmth and kindness helped many of us on a dark or rainy day,' he grinned and reached for her hand under the covers. 'Grandad felt responsible so he asked me to help you. He knew I liked you before I did, I think,' Liam admitted. 'But I didn't know how to help. You were never really "there" when you were at the café, so distant. Distracted. Then you'd just go home. But one day I found out about yoga in the trees and I thought being outdoors might help, so I posted the flyer into your letterbox,' he smiled a little shamefaced.

'I made it part of my morning routine to be the first through the door so you'd see a friendly face every day and I did my best to maintain Rose when you left her out on the street. I'd top her up with oil and check the windscreen wash. Small things, just so you didn't have to worry about them.' He shrugged as Mia began to comprehend all the little things he'd done for her the past year. 'And, um, a few months before Grandad died he told me two things.' Liam held his free hand up. 'One, where his stash of pink notelet cards were, and how important it was for you to keep hearing kind and inspiring things. And two, that he'd left something for you in his will.'

He sat, looking at her as Mia took everything in that he'd just told her. 'You can speak now,' he looked uneasily at her. Worried at her silence.

'It was you? You left the notes?' Suddenly it all began to make much more sense. 'But why didn't you say something? I had no idea who was sending them when Albert stopped visiting.' She paused, looking at Liam. 'But also, how didn't we spot the relationship? You both came to the café,' she said, hoping for an explanation.

'Wrong times. He always laughed at that, ships that passed and all that,' Liam said evenly. 'I was in early, as you know, and he was in 10.30am. Our routines just didn't intersect. And as far as telling you I liked you Mia,' Liam rolled his eyes. 'It's a lot easier to say something romantic when you can spend the evening writing it out, rather than trying to talk to you. You can be quite fierce sometimes,' he grinned.

'I can?' Mia was shocked. 'I don't mean to be.'

Liam leant in and kissed her on the cheek. 'I know. It's usually because you're busy, or, I suspect, thinking about the next cake you're decorating.' She grinned at his accuracy. 'But I am sorry I didn't tell you sooner that I liked you.' He looked away for a moment. 'I was gutted when I realised you were into Will,' he shook his head.

Mia bit her lip and moved closer to him to get his attention. 'I think I was just confused. It was the proximity thing. We were working together, it had been a while since Jake had left and I'd sworn off men. So, the first guy who seemed interested in me I did get a bit into,' she quickly carried on, sensing Liam's unease. 'But he *never* gave the impression he was into me. And now he's with Ellie, I definitely don't have any feelings like that for him.'

'Even when you thought he'd kissed you?' Liam leant in, kissing her on the mouth in the way that made her body sing.

'Frankly I decided whoever was behind that kiss I was going to be devoted to, if they could make me weak-kneed with a kiss, who knew what else they could do?' Mia said laughing as Liam began to tickle her. 'Okay. Honestly? I hoped it was you. With every bit of my body, but I was convinced you'd left early and didn't like me,' she smiled sadly. 'I thought I'd got the wrong idea about us, I've spent the last few weeks getting a lot wrong.

Liam traced her lips with his thumb. 'You're not getting the wrong idea about this, are you?' He leant in and kissed her. 'Because I really, really like you Mia Jones,' he kissed her on the neck and Mia beamed with pleasure.

'I can cope with that.'

Chapter Twenty-Three

'Ready?' Liam stood with Mia outside the solicitors. 'I can come in with you if you like?'

She felt nervous. She didn't know why, but Mia had always felt awkward in situations which called upon her to be a bit more grown-up. Garages had that effect. Hospitals. And solicitors. But she shook her head. 'No, I'll be okay. I'll call you when I'm out. Hopefully it'll be quick,' she smiled, kissed Liam on the cheek and turned on her heels to go in. She'd dressed smartly, though she felt a little like she was going to a funeral. Fairly apt though, she acknowledged, it was the reading of Albert's wishes for her. Whatever they were she felt he was owed a smart appearance.

After announcing herself to the receptionist who asked her to sit in the waiting room, Mia looked around noting the deep walnut walls, heavy oil paintings and sumptuous furnishings.

'Miss Jones?' A man came in, aged somewhere in his 50s, dressed in a well-cut pinstripe grey suit and bright white shirt and beckoned her into his office.

'Tea? Coffee?' he asked, as he indicated she sat down. Mia sat carefully on the edge of the warm brown leather seat and shook her head. She was nervous.

He smiled. 'Want to just get down to it? Fair enough. I'm Mr Portland, but you can call me Daniel. I believe you're here to find out what Mr Albert Sensale left you?'

Mia swallowed, she should have said yes to the offer of a drink. 'Yes,' she managed in a small voice. 'But I'm not expecting anything, this all feels a bit over the top to be honest,' she admitted, raising a smile from Daniel.

'Not to worry. Let's just have a read shall we?' He placed a pair of gold rimmed reading glasses on his nose and read the document in front of him that sat, amongst many other books and papers, on top of the oak desk. It was as though they'd had the same furnishings since the company opened 150 years ago. Mia smiled at the idea.

'Ah, a grin. Lovely,' Daniel smiled back. 'I think you'll be smiling even more now. Right, here it is.' He cleared his throat and began reading the last Will and Testament of Albert Sensale.

I wish to leave Mia Jones, who owns Tiers of Joy, the sum of £25,000. She was terribly kind to me and made every day this last year contain a moment of brightness. Us old folk don't come by those very often and I count myself very lucky that I found her. I hope this will help her, should the very likely need arise that she'll need to replace that rust bucket she favours so much in the not too distant future.

'Rust bucket?' Daniel smiled and Mia couldn't reply. She had a hard lump in her throat and tears in her eyes. The money was welcome, of course it was, but it was Albert's words which had got her. She could hear his voice and see his eyes twinkling with satisfaction that he'd fixed the Rose problem.

She shook her head. 'No? Not going to tell me?' Daniel smiled. 'Fair enough. Anyway, I'll get my PA to draw up the paperwork and we can get the funds transferred to you as quickly as possible,' he said, smiling still. 'You're very quiet, are you sure you're okay?' He looked concerned. 'Do you need a glass of water?'

Mia recovered herself. 'No, I'm...fine...just a bit shocked. I didn't know Albert all that well and that money, well, it's come at just the right time. But I'm a bit speechless,' she grinned.

Daniel's smile broadened. 'I often find that's the response. This is the nice part of the job,' he confided. 'No warring families.'

Mia laughed at his openness. 'Well, thank you. I'm thrilled – and getting more used to it.' She stood up and shook Daniel's hand. 'Thank you.'

Once she'd left the office, Mia allowed herself a moment to dance with happiness. She couldn't believe her luck and clicked on her phone to call Liam, then had another thought. Pressing call on another number in her phone, she grinned.

'Hi – Ted? It's Mia, we met yesterday?' She listened as the voice expressed delight at hearing from her so soon. 'I'd like to take you up on the offer for the camper van if it's still available,' she crossed her fingers and hoped Albert was watching over her. 'She is? Marvellous, yes please, and Ted, thank you. It'll be free cakes and coffee for you whenever you want. She finished the call then rang Liam, her mind whirring with possibilities for her mobile café.

'I'm across the street,' he said when he answered and she looked up. Standing there, his phone held to his ear in one hand and a large bunch of pink roses in his other, he grinned at her, his voice coming through the earpiece of her phone, whilst she watched him talk. 'It's a few days late, but I thought you'd like something from your *Secret Valentine*.'

Chapter Twenty Four

360 days later

'Happy Valentine's Day,' Ellie toasted Mia. They were sat amidst boxes that were half unpacked.

'Happy Valentine's,' said Liam, coming over with his plate loaded with Chinese food and finding somewhere to sit amongst the cushions and plants strewn around the place. 'Are you sure this place is going to be big enough for you? There's a lot of stuff here,' he said, grinning as Ellie threw a prawn cracker at him.

'I'll have you know Will has said he welcomes all the homely items I'm bringing with me, haven't you?' she said as Will came over with a bottle of wine.

'Yes, but that's when I didn't realise how *many* plants you had. It's like a greenhouse in here,' he said, laughing.

'I can move out again,' Ellie said, pouting.

'Absolutely not,' Mia said. 'You think you're going to have someone lift all this stuff again for you? You'll be on your own. No, you stay put, it's the right thing to do,' she nodded to Will for wine. 'Yes please. Your girlfriend is a hard taskmaster.'

'Don't I know it,' he said grinning. 'But she's my taskmaster and I wouldn't have it any other way,' he leant over to kiss Ellie, making Mia smile. The two had been inseparable the past year and she'd never seen her best friend so happy.

'Alright, get a room,' Mia said, laughing. 'Though, there's so many to choose from now you're lady of the manor, how will you choose?' Ellie moving in had coincided with Will's mum moving out after a whirlwind romance with a tech billionaire. Something that no one was disappointed with.

'How's the café Mia?' Will asked as they all fell on their food, starving from a day moving Ellie out of her flat and into the manor house.

Mia nodded, slurping a noodle up. 'Really well. I've got a pattern I've fallen into now and they all know where I'll be each day of the week. I love the different locations I stop in, and I meet such a variety of people,' she enthused. The last year had been tough. Setting up a brand new business was never going to be easy. Every day Mia had woken before dawn, taken the VW to a place in the county where she'd identified a need for a good cup of coffee and a natter, providing homemade cakes and plenty of chat to her regulars.

'She's doing herself down. I've seen her out there, working her socks off,' Liam said with pride. 'Most of her regulars are the older generation, the ones who live alone. For a lot of them when she turns up it's the high point of their week, a focal point for making friends and enjoying a cake. She's become a lifeline to a lot of them, I'm convinced of it.' He kissed Mia on the cheek.

Mia shook her head. 'I don't just cater to older people, I get a lot of mums of young children too. Turns out there are a lot of lonely people out there, it's nice to make them a little happier.'

'To Mia,' Ellie said, her face beaming with pride. In the early days when Mia was juggling the campervan renovation and numerous issues with her baking equipment, Ellie and Will had encouraged her to bake at the kitchen on site at the manor house, as long as she made a few extra for the café.

'And *Albert's*,' Mia reminded them. She'd broken with her tradition and named her campervan with a boy's name. She felt it was a celebration of the man who'd enabled her latest venture and a reminder of all the people who needed a little conversation in their lives.

'To *Albert's*,' the four chorused, taking large sips of wine to toast.

'You're sitting on a note,' Liam said, smiling at Mia. She frowned, and moved a little, spotting the pink notelet under her.

'What does it say?' she asked, her heart skipping a beat.

Liam grinned. 'What do you think?'

She opened the paper, aware of the three of them sat around her, their eyes on her and read the words he'd written carefully on a pink slip.

Will you marry me?

Mia looked back up from the paper.

'Well?' Liam said, kneeling in front of her with a vintage diamond and sapphire ring in his hand and a huge smile on his face.

Mia grinned.

'As long as I can make the cake.'

The End

Acknowledgements

Well, who knew when I mooted this idea of a "secret series" how well the first, Secret Santa, would do? I was blown away by the feedback I received, as it seemed to touch people in different ways. I had readers reaching out such as Shannon Porter who was so inspired by Secret Santa she wrote her own Christmas book for children off the back of it!

Thank you everyone who has read, reviewed and spread the (not so) secret word. I hope you enjoy this instalment. Feel free to message me on Instagram (holly_green_author) or Tik Tok (HollyGreenAuthor), as I love to hear what you think.

If you liked this book, give it a rating. Thank you.

Thanks to my incredible writing bestie, Daisy White. She's a writing force to be reckoned with and my go-to on everything. Thanks for saying this was good enough when I was losing hope with it. The difficult second album, eh?

Thanks to my very wonderful friends who have supported my writing including Hannah Stewart, Pam Nikiteas, Lis Briggs and Emma Jones. A special mention to thank Mia Jones for the use of her name (hope you don't mind there's a couple of kissing scenes).

Big kisses to my parents, sis and family who've been thrilled to see my books on sale and have been doing the best PR job for me.

Thanks once again to my husband who now "gets" the whole romcom thing, and agrees that yes, my watching of Hallmark and Richard Curtis movies is, in fact, research.

Massive thanks to my lovely son for all the teas and hugs, and of course, a special thank you to the marvellous Miss B, who is official proof-reader of all things Secret, and approves this novel.

Recipe

In my last novella, Secret Santa, I included some recipes which went down very well. In honour of that, and my *many* hours of research sat in cafés writing this whilst enjoying more than my fair share of cakes and biscuits, here's a recipe for Cinnamon Rolls, which feature very heavily in Secret Valentine. Enjoy!

Ingredients

300g self-raising flour
    2 tbsp caster sugar
    1 tsp ground cinnamon
    70g butter, melted, plus extra for greasing
    2 egg yolks
    130ml milk, plus extra for glazing

Filling

1 tsp ground cinnamon
    55g light brown soft sugar
    2 tbsp caster sugar
    40g butter, melted

Icing

60g icing sugar
  1 tbsp cream cheese, softened
  ½ tbsp butter, softened
  ½ tsp vanilla essence

Heat oven to 180C/fan 160C/gas 4. Grease a 20cm loose-bottomed cake tin and line the bottom with baking parchment. Mix the flour, caster sugar and cinnamon together with a pinch of salt in a bowl. Whisk the butter, egg yolks and milk together and combine with the dry ingredients to make a soft dough. Turn out onto a floured surface and roll out to a rectangle, about 30 x 25cm.

Mix the filling ingredients together. Spread evenly over the dough then roll it up lengthways so it looks like a log. Cut the dough with a sharp knife into eight even-sized slices and place in the tin. Brush with a little extra milk and bake for 30-35 mins or until golden brown (keep an eye after about 25 minutes). Remove from the oven and leave to cool for five minutes before you remove them from the tin.

Sift the icing sugar into a large bowl and make a well in the centre. Place the cream cheese and butter in the centre, pour over 2 tbsp boiling water. Then stir to mix. Add a little more water until it's relatively runny. Stir in the vanilla essence, then drizzle the icing over the rolls. Demolish.

About the Author

Holly loves a romance and is enjoying writing all the squishy, lovey, fun, twinkly stories she can think of!

As well as Hallmark Christmas movies and anything that Reese Witherspoon has either read, directed, acted in or produced, Holly enjoys reading all sorts of books, from adventures to YA, to sleuth mysteries and crime capers.

Her favourite kind of day is one which starts with a crisp, bright morning, where she gets to walk her dog for miles in the English countryside. Followed by a morning of writing, and an afternoon which revolves around massive hot chocolates, blankets and a good book.

When she starts writing, Holly tends to forget everything going on around her and immerses herself in all things made up. She lives in West Sussex with her two kids, husband and footwarmer (also known as a dog).

Also By

The Secret Series
Secret Santa
Secret Crush – coming Summer 2024

Printed in Great Britain
by Amazon